THE DARING
MARRIAGE

Barbara Cartland

Barbara Cartland Ebooks Ltd

This edition © 2023

ISBNs

9781782139836   EPUB

9781788676694   PAPERBACK

Book design by M-Y Books
m-ybooks.co.uk

THE BARBARA CARTLAND ETERNAL COLLECTION

The Barbara Cartland Eternal Collection is the unique opportunity to collect all five hundred of the timeless beautiful romantic novels written by the world's most celebrated and enduring romantic author.

Named the Eternal Collection because Barbara's inspiring stories of pure love, just the same as love itself, the books will be published on the internet at the rate of four titles per month until all five hundred are available.

The Eternal Collection, classic pure romance available worldwide for all time .

THE LATE DAME BARBARA CARTLAND

Barbara Cartland, who sadly died in May 2000 at the grand age of ninety eight, remains one of the world's most famous romantic novelists. With worldwide sales of over one billion, her outstanding 723 books have been translated into thirty six different languages, to be enjoyed by readers of romance globally.

Writing her first book 'Jigsaw' at the age of 21, Barbara became an immediate bestseller. Building upon this initial success, she wrote continuously throughout her life, producing bestsellers for an astonishing 76 years. In addition to Barbara Cartland's legion of fans in the UK and across Europe, her books have always been immensely popular in the USA. In 1976 she achieved the unprecedented feat of having books at numbers 1 & 2 in the prestigious B. Dalton Bookseller bestsellers list.

Although she is often referred to as the 'Queen of Romance', Barbara Cartland also wrote several historical biographies, six autobiographies and numerous theatrical plays as well as books on life, love, health and cookery. Becoming one of Britain's most popular media personalities and dressed in her trademark pink, Barbara spoke on radio and television about social and political issues, as well as making many public appearances.

In 1991 she became a Dame of the Order of the British Empire for her contribution to literature and her work for humanitarian and charitable causes.

Known for her glamour, style, and vitality Barbara Cartland became a legend in her own lifetime. Best remembered for her wonderful romantic novels and loved by millions of readers worldwide, her books remain treasured for their heroic heroes, plucky heroines and traditional values. But above all, it was Barbara Cartland's overriding belief in the positive power of love to help, heal and improve the quality of life for everyone that made her truly unique.

AUTHOR'S NOTE

As I explained in this novel, from 1873 onwards, the Russians were influenced and excited and by the idea of a 'Slavic Federation' with Russia at its head and with its Capital in Constantinople'.

The Czarina, particularly, looked on it as a Religious Crusade, a chance to alleviate the lot of the oppressed Balkan Christians.

It was also a good chance to bring back the great Church of Santa Sophia to its rightful Orthodoxy and re-establish Constantinople as the greatest City in Christendom.

A revolt in the Turkish Province of Herzegovina in the summer of 1875 set the first sparks flying and a year later Serbia declared war on Turkey and scores of Russian volunteers poured into Belgrade.

Soon after the outbreak of the Serbian War, stories began to filter back into the European Press of an uprising in Bulgaria that had been put down by terrible Turkish reprisals.

It was said that sixty villages were destroyed and twelve thousand people slaughtered.

It was not until Queen Victoria had had her way and the presence of the British Navy alarmed Grand Duke Nicholas so that the Russians, who had advanced to within six miles of Constantinople, were forced to withdraw.

CHAPTER ONE
1875

The door opened and a clerk formally announced,

"The Earl of Derby, Prime Minister."

Mr. Disraeli then rose to his feet as the Secretary of State for Foreign Affairs advanced towards him.

"How are you?" he asked.

"Well, thank you," the Earl replied, "but I am sure that you have bad news or you would not have sent for me at this unearthly hour."

The Prime Minister laughed.

Having a fine sense of humour himself, he always enjoyed the wit of his contemporaries.

Unfortunately some of them took life very seriously and seldom smiled let alone laughed at the difficulties that constantly confronted Parliament.

The Earl of Derby next sat down on a chair at the other side of the Prime Minister's desk.

"What has gone wrong now?" he asked.

There was undoubtedly a wary note in his voice.

"I hate to tell you," the Prime Minister answered, "but Her Majesty sent for me yesterday to say that she has received an urgent request from King Hadrian of Arginos."

He paused and, seeing the expression in the eyes of the Foreign Secretary, he added,

"I think you may have guessed already what she requires."

The Earl of Derby held up his hands.

"Not again," he answered. "I just cannot bear it."

"I knew you would feel like that," Mr. Disraeli said, "but Her Majesty is the one person who seems to realise the seriousness of what is now happening in the Balkans. The King, not unnaturally, desires the support of Great Britain to prevent what he says is the infiltration of the Russians, who are making considerable trouble in that part of the world."

"If he wants to marry off one of his children to a relative of Queen Victoria, I can tell you here and now that it is quite impossible," the Earl declared firmly. "We have used up every one of her very many relatives until there literally is not a cousin, however distant, left unmarried."

The irritated tone of his voice made the Prime Minister laugh again.

"It is no use," he said, "you know what Her Majesty is like when she has made up her mind and, although she has twenty-two or twenty-three, I have forgotten which, relatives on the Thrones of Europe, she is determined to have one more. And you will have to find her!"

The Earl threw up his hands in a helpless gesture.

"I cannot manufacture this young woman out of thin air," he complained, "and, while we are talking about it, I am trying to remember just where Arginos is."

The Prime Minister then produced a map from a drawer in his desk.

"It is North of Greece," he said, "and was at one time part of that country. It is now at the very end of Livadia, an Independent State that was most fortunately not swallowed up by the Ottoman Empire."

"And what is the trouble?" the Earl enquired.

"Need you ask?" the Prime Minister replied. "Russia is determined to take over what she can of the Balkans. I am told as well that she has her eyes on Constantinople as well."

"I have heard that," the Earl responded sharply.

He spoke testily as if the Prime Minister was poaching on his particular preserve.

"I can only hope that it is not true," Mr. Disraeli went on, "but a friend of mine who was in Russia only a week or so ago told me that in St. Petersburg they are all influenced by two books. One is a nineteen-page brochure written by a General Fadeyev, the son of a former Governor. The other one is a long treatise called *Russia and Europe* by Nicholas Danilevsky, a Civil Servant."

"How does that concern any of the Politicians who bother to read them?" the Earl asked.

"The trouble is that both of the books glorify War and they hold up as a goal a Slavic Federation with Russia as its head."

Mr. Disraeli paused.

Then he added in an impressive tone,

"And its Capital would be Constantinople."

The Earl of Derby sat upright in his chair.

"I don't believe it! The idea is dangerous and, of course, simply ridiculous."

"The Russians certainly don't think so," the Prime Minister said quietly, "and it appeals to everybody, especially the Czarina."

The Earl of Derby drew in his breath.

"The Empress?" he queried.

"She looks on it as if it is a religious Crusade," the Prime Minister said, "and wishes to establish Constantinople as the greatest City in Christendom."

"The whole idea is preposterous!" the Earl exclaimed.

"I wish it was," the Prime Minister said, "but on this I agree with Her Majesty, that the situation in the Balkans is something that we must deeply consider in every aspect."

He knew, as he spoke, that the Earl of Derby was not convinced.

Put forward it did sound an exaggerated idea and yet Russia was always unpredictable and sinister.

Both the Prime Minister and the Foreign Secretary were aware that the Russians were stirring up as much trouble as they could in the Balkans.

This had resulted in the Balkans, wherever it was possible, wanting a close connection with Great Britain.

The easiest way to ensure that this was so was to marry their King or Crown Prince to one of Queen Victoria's relations.

As the Earl had said, this source was beginning to dry up or, as he believed, was already exhausted.

Both men were silent for a moment.

Then the Prime Minister asked,

"There must be somebody to fill the bill and, although the situation may not be as serious as we might think, it could surely prevent Russia from infiltrating any further into the other countries South of Macedonia."

"I am almost certain," the Earl of Derby said, "that unless Her Majesty has someone 'up her sleeve' there are no more relatives and King Hadrian will have to look elsewhere."

"Where can he look?" the Prime Minister queried beneath his breath.

Both men were aware that the only country for whom Russia had any respect was Great Britain.

With her enormous resources, Russia could in fact very easily overrun all the countries that bordered the Black Sea.

It would be exceedingly difficult for any European Power to even try to stop her.

At the same time the Czar of Russia, Alexander II, was a man who appreciated peace. He had no wish to go to war with anybody.

As if the Earl of Derby was following the Prime Minister's thoughts, he next said,

"The Russian Army is not mobilised for war and I do not believe that the Czar will allow it."

"I was talking to someone who has just been in Russia who told me that it is true," the Prime Minister remarked, "but the Grand Duke Nicholas, who has the keen support of the Czarina, is eager to secure more territories for Russia and prove himself a National Hero."

There was silence until the Prime Minister commented,

"I have no wish to return to Her Majesty the Queen and say we have failed to produce what she requires."

"Surely there must be someone who can marry the King?" the Earl remarked.

"It is not the King," Mr. Disraeli replied. "He already has a wife. No, it is not quite as bad as that. It is his second son, Prince Darius, who is free to take a bride. His elder brother is married."

"You surely don't believe that some 'two-penny-half-penny' Prince we have never heard of," the Earl of Derby asked scornfully, "is going to deter the Russians from attempting to annexe Constantinople?"

"No, but it will prevent them from creating a Revolution in Arginos," the Prime Minister said quietly, "which is what they have done in other parts of the Balkans. I do not know whether you are aware of the chaos they have caused in the North, but I feel we should try to do something to prevent their greed swallowing up these small independent States that are, because there are so many of them, a safeguard against complete Russian domination of the whole region."

"I see your reasoning, Prime Minister," the Earl answered, "but I still cannot produce a bride out of thin air if, quite simply, the girl does not exist."

"I have to agree with you there," the Prime Minister said. "I suppose you are prepared to give the bad news to Her Majesty?"

The Earl threw up his hands.

"God forbid! That is your job!"

"On the contrary," Mr. Disraeli said with a twinkle in his eyes. "*You* are the Foreign Secretary!"

"Dammit all!" the Earl swore. "You ask too much."

He spoke with ferocious exasperation.

Then, as he met the Prime Minister's eyes, they both laughed.

"I know your methods only too well," the Earl said. "You are making this a challenge so that I shall have to comb the country from North to South, rather than face Her Majesty with failure."

They were both well aware how disagreeable the Queen could be if her orders were not fully carried out.

The Earl was thinking that the only person who could handle her was the Prime Minister himself.

He had a charming ingratiating manner, which inevitably delighted her.

It was well known by all the Ministries that she favoured Benjamin Disraeli and disliked, almost with a deep sense of naked hostility, Mr. Gladstone, the Leader of the Opposition in Parliament.

The Earl thought with horror how unpleasant the interview would be if he had to tell Her Majesty that there was no bride for Prince Darius.

Therefore the King of Arginos's request for help must regrettably remain unanswered.

"I tell you what we will do," the Prime Minister suggested unexpectedly. "We will ask Smithson, who is in charge of the Genealogy of Europe. There may perhaps be a daughter of one of the Queen's relatives who is already on a Throne."

"That is a good idea, Benjamin," the Earl exclaimed, looking much more cheerful.

As the Prime Minister finished speaking, he rang a bell.

When the door opened, he ordered,

"Send Mr. Smithson to me at once."

The door closed and the Earl said,

"I have never known you to be beaten by anything you undertook. I am only praying now that someone will turn up, although God knows who."

"One never knows one's luck," the Prime Minister replied.

The door opened and George Smithson came in.

He was a middle-aged man whose hair was just beginning to turn grey.

He bowed politely both to the Prime Minister and then to the Earl of Derby.

"I sent for you, Smithson," the Prime Minister said, "because we have a difficult problem we have to solve. Her Majesty the Queen has been requested by King Hadrian of Arginos to provide a suitable bride, who is also one of Her Majesty's relatives, for his second son.

The Foreign Secretary, the Earl of Derby, and I have found it completely impossible to think of anyone available."

George Smithson was silent.

Both men were aware that for the last three years he had been working on the Genealogy of Europe.

Nobody else had such a vast knowledge of the various reigning Sovereigns, Princes and Grand Dukes who were of the 'Blood Royal'.

They waited patiently, no one making a sound.

Both the Prime Minister and the Earl were aware that George Smithson was mentally looking back over pages upon pages of Family Trees, which filled the shelves in his office to capacity.

Finally the Earl began to fidget.

He was thinking that Smithson would only confirm what he and the Prime Minister knew already, that it was really impossible for Great Britain to provide a bride for Arginos.

Then George Smithson said slowly,

"There is, Prime Minister, just the one young lady available who is connected with Her Majesty the Queen."

The Earl sat upright.

"There is one? Who?"

"She is, my Lord," George Smithson replied, "Lady Gloria Winton, daughter of the Duke of Norwinton."

Both men stared at him until the Prime Minister exclaimed,

"Of course! The Duchess was the Princess Caroline of Lichenberg."

"But she renounced the title when she married the Duke," the Earl added.

"She may have done," the Prime Minister agreed, "but Smithson is right. Lady Gloria, through her mother, is, of course, slightly related to Her Majesty. No one can deny that."

There was silence before the Earl of Derby said,

"And you really think that King Hadrian will accept Lady Gloria?"

"It is a question of his taking what he is offered or going without," the Prime Minister said. "And Smithson can very easily make out a Family Tree that will be impressive enough for Arginos."

"I as well think, my Lord," George Smithson said, "there must be some Royal relatives, however distant, in the Duke's lineage."

"Well, make them just as impressive as you can," the Prime Minister said. "Of course the Duchess's claim as a relation of the Queen, albeit very distant, is totally valid."

"Of course, Prime Minister, that is very true," George Smithson said. "I will get to work immediately."

He bowed politely and went from the room.

As the door closed behind him, the Earl sighed,

"He is a genius. I had completely forgotten that the Duchess of Norwinton could claim any relationship to the Queen."

"So had I," the Prime Minister admitted. "After all, you do not see them at Court very often. The Duke prefers to be on his estate in the North and I have no idea what the girl actually looks like."

"Whatever she is like," the Earl said firmly, "she is exactly what the King has asked for and, even if she is as plain as a pikestaff, Prince Darius will have to welcome her with open arms."

He rose as he spoke.

"Tell Her Majesty," he said, "that I will get in touch with the Ambassador of Arginos immediately. I would suppose that the bride will want a Battleship to take her to Arginos for the Wedding."

"You go too fast," the Prime Minister said. "We can only speculate that there will be a Wedding. Unless Her Majesty is determined to raise the Union Jack in the Russians' faces before they take a step further."

"I expect that is just what she does intend," the Earl said, "but I leave it to you, Prime Minister, to find out. You are far better at it than I am."

He rose as he spoke and then said,

"I think, having solved one of the knottiest problems I have had for some time, we might have a drink on it. There is some champagne in my office, or a glass of brandy, which you might even enjoy more."

"Very well," the Prime Minister said, "I will join you and I think, very frankly, that we deserve it."

*

The Duke of Norwinter's estate was a very large one in the Southern part of the County of Yorkshire.

His Castle, which was magnificent, had been built over four centuries earlier and added to by every succeeding generation of the family.

The Duke had often thought, with his great rolling acres of excellent land, that he was a King in a small Kingdom all of his own.

The fact that he had married a Royal Princess added to the Duke's fantasy.

The Duke was an extremely handsome man.

He had fallen in love with Princess Caroline of Lichenberg when he was travelling in her father's country.

She was exceptionally beautiful and was already being pursued by several Princes from neighbouring countries.

However, once she had seen the Duke, then the Earl of Winton, she lost her heart and no other man ever existed.

But they had had to fight desperately to be allowed to marry.

They might, in point of fact, have been refused permission had the Earl not come into the Dukedom.

Also, the Princess's father suddenly became extremely ill.

It was therefore easier to give in to her pleadings that she might marry an Englishman.

She would rather renounce her title than continue to moon about The Palace in tears.

She was, however, helped by the fact that she had three older brothers.

Then there were her two older sisters, who had both suitably married other Rulers of Principalities, but tragically the two girls had been exceedingly unhappy.

This made the Queen decide that the youngest and least important of her children should be allowed to marry the man she loved.

"I love Richard, I love him, *I love him, Mama*!" the Princess had cried desperately. "If you will not let me marry him, I swear I will go into a Convent or kill myself!"

"Don't be so theatrical," the Queen corrected her sharply.

At the same time she deeply sympathised with her daughter.

She herself had not been particularly happy in her arranged marriage.

It was not surprising, considering she had been only eighteen when she had married the King of Lichenberg.

He was nearly fifty and had been married before to a woman who had provided him with only daughters but no sons.

Finally, Princess Caroline's marriage was allowed on condition that she renounces her title.

After that she was no longer considered Royal.

It did not matter one iota to the Princess.

All she wanted was to be the wife of the man she had given her heart to.

She would have felt the same about him whether he was a Duke or a chimney-sweep.

They were blissfully happy together.

The Duchess had, however, always stipulated that no child of hers should be forced to marry for Political reasons.

She could never forget just how miserable her poor sisters had been.

When she had gone to England, she had, to all intents and purposes, lost touch with her family.

She did hear about them from time to time.

Yet, as she and the Duke were just so happy, they seldom went to Court and any news of Lichenberg came mostly from the newspapers.

After her father and mother were both dead, the Princess altogether lost touch with her relatives.

Her elder brother, now King, had married a fat German Princess.

She would, the Duchess knew, despise anyone who could give up their Royal status to become a commoner.

"Why should we want to be with anyone but ourselves, Richard?" the Duchess asked not once but a thousand times.

The Duke invariably agreed with her.

When they had a family of their own, he had no wish to go to London or anywhere else.

He knew that people would make a fuss of his wife simply because they were impressed by her Royal blood.

Instead they travelled to Scotland and visited many different parts of Europe.

Their first child was a girl.

Because she had a head of golden hair and was beautiful, even as a baby, they called her 'Gloria'.

After Gloria came two sons, which naturally thrilled the Duke. They were also adored by their mother.

It was an incredibly happy family that lived at Winton Castle, delightfully content to be by themselves, rather than surrounded by people.

The Duke soon realised, as his daughter grew older, that she was very intelligent.

He had an extremely astute brain himself and he therefore greatly enjoyed teaching her the Classics and often other subjects that she did not learn from her Governesses.

As the boys grew older, the Duke decided that they must have a highly qualified Tutor.

Because it made things easier, the Tutor also taught Gloria and this meant that she was given a boy's education.

At the same time she learnt a great deal from her mother that was not obtainable from books.

The Duchess decided that she would present Gloria to Queen Victoria at her Court just before her eighteenth birthday.

Unfortunately, the Duke's mother, who had been in ill health for quite some years, died and they were therefore plunged into deep mourning.

So Gloria's visit to London and the Season had to be cancelled.

She remained at The Castle in Yorkshire.

"I am sorry, my darling. You must have been looking forward to it," the Duchess tried to console her.

"To tell the truth, Mama, I would much rather be here," Gloria replied to her. "It was unbearable for me to think of leaving our wonderful horses."

The Duchess had laughed.

She knew that her husband and her daughter were happiest when they were in the saddle and the same applied to the two boys.

She herself liked riding, but she was not obsessed by it.

Yet, as she told her husband,

"If it makes you happy always to be riding on a horse, then I must join you or be left behind."

Gloria had to miss the balls, Receptions and Assemblies that she was to have attended in London as a *debutante*.

But she never missed a meeting of the hounds and she loved watching her father's horses run on the more notable Racecourses in the North.

She was the winner at every Point-to-Point in which ladies were permitted to compete.

It was when their long year of mourning ended that the Duchess again began to plan a visit to London.

"I wonder if I will enjoy it as much as you think I will, Mama," Gloria said wistfully. "The money you are expending on my clothes could buy us three or four superb new horses."

"Your father can see to all that," the Duchess replied. "I am determined that you and I will be properly dressed, even if they do look upon us as 'Country Bumpkins'!"

Gloria laughed.

Her mother was so lovely and so charming that no one could possibly describe her as a 'Country Bumpkin'.

She had no idea that she herself was exquisite.

The gentlemen who saw her out hunting or riding thought that they must be dreaming when they saw her

Everything was arranged for them to travel to London in the middle of April.

Meanwhile Gloria was, of course, spending every moment she possibly could with her beloved horses.

She rode through the woods, looking at all the green leaves now beginning to appear on the boughs of the trees.

The bluebells and daffodils growing beneath them were lovelier this year than she ever remembered.

She turned her horse for home.

As she came within sight of The Castle, she was surprised to see a smart carriage on the drive and it was drawn by four well-bred horses.

She wondered for a few moments who it was calling on her father.

She thought that the horses looked rather tired as if they had been driven a long way and speedily.

A footman opened the door to her and, as she walked into the hall, she asked,

"Who is here, Henry?"

"It be a gentleman from London, my Lady, has called to see 'His Grace."

"From London!" Gloria exclaimed in some surprise.

Her father seldom received any visitors from London.

However, a great number of people in the country counted on his support for one project or another.

Gloria was about to go upstairs to change her clothes when the butler appeared.

"His Grace has been waiting for you to return, my Lady," he said. "He be in the study."

"Thank you, Armstrong, I expected that he will be in his study and I will go there now."

Wondering how her father's visitor from London could in any way concern her, Gloria pulled off her riding hat and placed it on a chair in the hall.

Then she walked slowly towards the study.

A footman opened the door for her and she went in.

Her father was standing, as he often did in his study, with his back to the fireplace.

Seated in one of the armchairs was an elderly and distinguished-looking man.

"Ah, there you are, Gloria," the Duke exclaimed. "You are later back to the house than I had thought."

"I have been as far as the beacon, Papa. It was such a lovely day that it seemed a pity to waste a single second of it."

The Duke smiled as if he knew exactly what she was thinking and he himself had no wish to leave Winton and go to London.

The man in the armchair had risen and now the Duke said to him,

"This, Your Excellency, is my daughter, Gloria. Gloria, dearest, this is His Excellency, the Ambassador of Arginos."

*

Some time afterwards, when Gloria went to her room, she found it difficult to remember exactly what had happened.

She was only conscious of a severe sense of shock.

She had been informed, and it seemed to her extremely abruptly, that she was to marry Prince Darius of Arginos because it was the wish of Queen Victoria.

"No – no – of course – not," she said quickly when she was told what was expected of her.

It was then that she had seen the expression in her father's eyes.

It had made her feel as if a cold hand had clasped her heart.

Now, at least, she was alone except for her lady's maid, who was helping her out of her riding habit.

She thought that she must have certainly imagined the whole thing.

How could it be possible that, before she could even be presented at Court, she would be married off?

And to some obscure Prince from a small Kingdom she knew nothing about and indeed had never even heard of!

The Ambassador had explained to her why he had come to The Castle.

She had expected her father to say politely that the whole idea was totally impossible.

He should have thanked His Excellency for coming so far and then asked him to kindly inform His Majesty the King of Arginos that the answer was very definately 'no'.

Unbelievably and astoundingly her father had said nothing like that.

Gloria suddenly had the terrifying feeling that prison walls were in inexorably closing in on her and she would then be unable to make a escape.

Finally her father suggested that she should go upstairs and change her clothes.

Without speaking a word she had hurried from the room as if she was being pursued by a thousand devils.

She was breathless by the time she reached her bedroom.

Now, she told herself, she had exaggerated the whole thing and there was no need for her to be afraid.

'Of course I cannot marry a man I have never seen, a man I know nothing about! A man who lives in some primitive country and most people would never know even where it was.'

But, why, why had her father not insisted firmly that the whole idea was ridiculous and absurd?

And why, when he had sent her up to change, had he said,

"We will talk about this later."

'There is nothing to talk about!' she raged to herself.

Vaguely, at the back of her mind, she had dreamt of being married.

One day, she thought, she would meet a man who would love her as much as her father loved her mother.

She knew only too well that they had had to fight to be allowed to marry.

And it had always seemed very romantic to Gloria.

"Did you really fall in love with Papa as soon as you saw him, Mama?" she would ask.

"He was the most handsome man I had ever seen in my whole life and, when I touched his hand, I knew that there was something between us that made us inseparable from each other," the Duchess replied.

"And Papa fell in love with you at the same time?" Gloria asked quietly.

Because it was so like a Fairytale, she had questioned her father.

"I went to see Lichenberg simply because the history of the country fascinated me," he related and I knew that it had some pictures I particularly wanted to see and then buy."

"So you obtained an introduction to the King?"

"It was not difficult," her father replied, "because he was so keen on racing. He had met my father on various Racecourses and he had asked him to come and stay in his country."

"And your father did not want to go, but you did," Gloria suggested.

"I went to Arginos and the first person I saw there was your mother."

"Was she very beautiful?"

"So beautiful that I felt she could not be real," he said simply. "And you, my darling, are very like her."

"I would like to think so," Gloria had replied. "I do hope, Papa, that I shall have such a romantic story as yours to tell when I get married."

"I am sure that the right man will come along," the Duke said. "But be careful not to be deceived by the wrong ones,"

"I will make certain of that," Gloria had replied.

She changed from her riding habit into a pretty gown that the Duchess had ordered from London for her.

Some of her clothes came from York.

Yet the Duchess was really determined that Gloria should shine in London Society and had sent for a number of gowns in the very latest fashion.

She looked so exquisitely lovely in them that the Duke said proudly to his wife,

"I am quite certain that Gloria will outshine every other *debutante* when you present her to Queen Victoria at Buckingham Palace."

"I would hope so," the Duchess replied, "but I am afraid that she will never find a man as handsome or as wonderful as you."

The Duke had put his arms round his wife and kissed her.

"Can you really think like that after we have been married for so long?"

"I love you much more now than when we first married," the Duchess replied, "and there is no other man in the whole world for me except for you."

The Duke knew that this was how he felt about his wife.

He kissed her with a passion that had grown rather than decreased with the years.

It made them both feel very young.

*

Gloria took one last look in the mirror before she went downstairs.

She was not in the least interested in her appearance.

She was only worrying how she could convince the Ambassador of Arginos that she had no intention of marrying the King's younger son.

'I am going to marry someone I love!' she told herself firmly as she reached the hall.

She walked towards the drawing room, where she knew that her father and mother would be entertaining the Ambassador.

As she did so, she suddenly felt afraid.

Supposing they had already accepted his ridiculous proposition?

Supposing they told her that she could not refuse the Prince even though he was not there to put the proposal to her himself?

Abruptly she told herself that she need not be afraid.

Non one could make her marry a man she did not wish to marry.

Her father and mother both knew that she wanted to fall in love as they had.

She wanted to love somebody until nothing else mattered, not even being a Princess of Royal Blood.

'They can surely find someone else who would be only too willing to marry the Prince,' she told herself as she walked into the drawing room.

CHAPTER TWO

To Gloria's surprise her father was alone in the drawing room.

"I want to talk to you, my dearest," he began as she sat down on the sofa by the window.

She looked at him warily, feeling that it was somewhat strange that there was no one else present.

"Before you start, Papa," she said quickly, "I want to make it quite clear that I have no intention of marrying Prince Darius, whom I have never met. You know you and Mama have always said that you did not approve of arranged marriages."

"I know," the Duke agreed quietly, "but the position now is rather different."

"In what way?" Gloria asked him resolutely.

She could not keep her voice from sounding hostile.

Her father took her hand and then sat down beside her on the sofa to say,

"You know that I married your mother despite a great deal of opposition from her father, the King, and, because I was afraid that she might incur criticism in England for marrying me, I gave up my duties at Court."

Gloria had not been completely aware of this, but she then asked him,

"Because you wanted to?"

"Of course I was so glad to do anything that would make your mother happy," the Duke replied, "and not feeling that she had done anything wrong in marrying me because she loved me."

Before Gloria could say a word, he went on,

"The situation now is that Queen Victoria has given her consent to your marriage and the Ambassador tells me that there is nobody, absolutely nobody else, who can save Arginos as they are asking you to do."

"Save them? From what?" Gloria enquired. "I am sure that they are making a fuss about nothing."

"I wish that was true," the Duke said, "but the Russians are very determined to establish themselves in the Balkans. It is well known that they are stirring up trouble in every small Principality. When there is a Revolution, it is considered a good excuse for them to go in to 'restore order'."

He saw something like a look of incredulity in his daughter's face and he went on,

"That means, of course, that the country will stay under Russian domination even though in some cases they put on the Throne a puppet who is completely under their thumb and does what he is told to do or face unpleasant consequences."

"Even if that is true, why should it worry us – in England?" Gloria asked. "What have we got to do with the Balkans?"

"Her Majesty the Queen is very afraid, and in my view quite rightly, that the Balance of Power, so important politically, will be upset if the Russians not only capture a great deal of the Balkans, but also try to establish themselves in Constantinople."

Gloria stared at him.

"How can they possibly do all that?"

"It is talked about quite openly in St. Petersburg," the Duke said. "And I have heard it from other sources besides the rumours being confirmed to me by the Ambassador."

There was a poignant silence.

Then Gloria said,

"I cannot believe that this is happening! Are you really trying to tell me, Papa, that I have to marry Prince Darius?"

The Duke rose to his feet and walked across to the mantelpiece.

He stood for a moment looking down into the fire.

And then he turned round.

"To be quite truthful, my beloved daughter," he said, "I am being selfish. I gave up, as I have already told you, my position at Court because I wanted to do so. But I wish William, as my eldest son, to eventually take his rightful place there."

"Are you trying to tell me," Gloria asked him, "that, if I refuse to marry Prince Darius, the Queen, if she is angry with me, will also extend her wrath to poor William, who is not yet seventeen?"

"I can say in all honesty," the Duke replied, "that if Her Majesty is thwarted, she might ostracise us as a family and that, my darling, makes me feel fearful!"

"I just don't believe it!" Gloria exclaimed. "How could she be so petty-minded?"

"The Balance of Power in Europe at this time is not in any way a petty problem," the Duke answered, "and Arginos, small though it might be, has a coastline on the Aegean Sea, where our Battleships have no difficulty at the moment in preserving the peace."

Gloria felt as if every word her father spoke was like a band of steel over her heart.

He was forcing her to become a prisoner of the Political world, which had never intruded into her life before.

She was intelligent enough to know that what her father was saying was indeed the truth.

Also that he was not exaggerating the importance and menace of the Russian threat.

Although the Duke seldom went to London, quite a number of his friends came to stay at The Castle. In this way he was able to keep reasonably up to date with all the latest news coming out of Europe.

Any Politician in London would have been surprised at what Gloria herself knew about foreign affairs and the ambitions of the Russians.

They were usually of no particular interest to a young girl.

She had listened to her father talking to her mother of the rising strength of the Russians in Europe and beyond.

She knew too that anyone concerned with India was aware that they were causing trouble on the North-West Frontier.

'Russians! Always the Russians,' she thought. 'Why should they interfere – in my life?'

Yet that was exactly what Russia was doing.

She was therefore wondering frantically how she could change her father's mind about this proposed marriage.

She wished only to stay in her beloved England and be of no importance to the Queen, the Prime Minister or Lord Derby.

Nor, for that matter, to the Ambassador of Arginos, who was waiting for her decision in another room.

"I know, my beautiful daughter, that this is not only a surprise, but also a shock," the Duke was saying. "I really cannot think how I can extricate you from such an uncomfortable position without incurring the wrath of Her Majesty."

"Surely there is somebody else available who could – marry the Prince?" Gloria asked in a very small voice.

"The Ambassador assures me," her father now explained, "that the Prime Minister and the Earl of Derby, who is the present Secretary of State for Foreign Affairs, were in despair until somebody in the office remembered that your mother is of Royal Blood."

"Surely Mama could think of – someone else who would be equally – suitable?" Gloria asked him plaintively.

"I have already talked to your mother about it," he replied, "and she has tried, I promise you, to think of somebody else who would be acceptable."

"But – I cannot do it – Papa – I *cannot*!" Gloria insisted forcefully.

Her father did not answer. He merely looked at her.

She knew that, because her two brothers were involved, he would not defend her.

She rose to her feet and walked over to the window.

Looking out at the garden she loved, she knew that it was something precious that she would have to leave behind.

There would also be the superb horses and everything that was home and family.

The Duke waited.

There was a sad expression in his eyes because he loved his daughter.

He knew only too well that what he was asking was an intolerable sacrifice on her part.

At the same time for the sake of his sons, he knew that he had to persuade her to do what the Queen expected.

Finally, after what had seemed a long time, Gloria turned round.

"Very well, Papa," she said. "For your sake and that of the boys, I will marry Prince Darius. *I hate him*! I hate him with every breath I draw, with every thought I think, because he is taking from me – my whole world – the world I love so much."

Her voice broke on the last words.

She ran to her father as if she was a child seeking his protection and reassurance.

The Duke put his arms round her and held her close.

"Thank you, my darling," he said. "Thank you for doing what is right. I can only pray that God will help you as I am unable to do myself."

*

Once Gloria realised that there was no way of escape from her Fate, she took no further interest in Arginos or the man she was to marry.

She allowed her father to make the necessary arrangements with the Ambassador without even asking what they were.

When finally His Excellency left, she learned, without showing the slightest emotion, that she was to leave for Arginos in three weeks.

"But, darling, it is seriously impossible to put together a trousseau in that short time," the Duchess complained.

Gloria made no complaints.

Nor did she take any interest in the dressmakers who were summoned to The Castle, not only from York but also from London.

She merely spent as much time as she could her time riding, sometimes with her father and sometimes alone.

She tried not to think of Prince Darius and she refused to take any interest in the history of his country that she was being forced to go to.

Nor would she open any of the books that her father procured for her at some expense.

When she learned that her father and mother were not going with her to Arginos, she did, however, protest vigorously,

"How can you both be so cruel? I really cannot be married to anyone unless you are both there to support and comfort me."

"Queen Victoria is sending one of her Ladies-of-the-Bedchamber to represent her at the Wedding, which will be a very grand one," the Duke replied, "and the Marquis of Garth, her husband, who is an old friend of mine, will accompany her."

He paused and as Gloria did not speak, he went on,

"You will also have the British Ambassador and his wife, who are coming over from Arginos to escort you and you will all travel in a British Battleship, which is being provided by the Earl of Derby."

"But – I don't want to go without – you and Mama," Gloria asserted pathetically.

"I know, my darling," the Duchess answered, "but your father has so many appointments here in the country and, because he thinks that the King of Arginos might reproach me and criticise me publicly for giving up my Royal title, it is best that we stay at home."

"The one person who is not being considered in this absurd charade," Gloria said angrily, "is me!"

She then walked out of the room, slamming the door behind her.

The Duchess looked at her husband.

"How can we let her suffer in this way?" she asked him again.

"I don't want to upset you," he replied, "but, as I have said to you before, my beloved wife, I am afraid that Gloria will be very unhappy or even hysterical just before the marriage takes place. If we are not there, she will be forced to have more control over herself. My decision is certainly in her very best interests."

"I understand exactly what you are saying," the Duchess answered. "At the same time Gloria is very sensitive and, because she had not been brought up as a Royal person, she does not understand, as I did, how important this sort of arrangement really is."

She spread out her hands in a helpless gesture as she went on,

"Royalty are just useful pawns in a Political game. They are not supposed to have hearts or feelings as individuals."

"I know that," the Duke said. "That is why, although it does seem cruel, our daughter is having to pay for our happiness. Nobody could have been as happy over the years as I have been with you."

"Or I with you," the Duchess said softly.

*

When she was alone in her bedroom, Gloria had to force herself not to cry.

She dreaded the future.

She tried not to think of the man who was waiting in a strange country to make her his wife.

'*I hate him*!' she told herself when she said a final 'goodbye' to her horses and felt that her heart was breaking.

"*I hate him*!" she said aloud over and over again as she drove down the drive, knowing it would be a long time before she saw The Castle again.

A great deal of her trousseau was waiting for her at Winton House in London.

She refused, however, to take any interest in it.

She was cold and indifferent to the compliments that were paid her by the people who called as soon as the Duke and Duchess arrived.

There were not only the members of the Arginosian Embassy that she had to meet, there was also the Earl of Derby, who brought with him a number of distinguished Statesmen and Politicians.

They wished to impress upon Gloria the really important role she had to play in Arginos because she was representing Great Britain and everything that Great Britain stood for.

She sat on a sofa in the drawing room listening to them politely as they droned on.

She, however, contributed as little to the conversation as possible.

She deliberately did not ask them any questions. The Duke, who knew how astute and active her brain was, had to ask them for her.

'I am not in the least interested in Arginos,' Gloria told herself when the guests finally departed, 'and, if they think that I can keep away the Russians single-handed, then they must be half-witted!'

The Duke realised at once exactly what she was thinking and feeling.

He therefore talked to her quietly when they were alone about the Political situation not just in the Balkans but all over the Continent.

He also talked to her about King Hadrian.

"The King, like most of his subjects, is principally Greek," he told her. "His father came from a very old Greek family and became King unexpectedly when two of those in direct line to the Throne were killed fighting for their country."

Gloria made no comment as usual and he carried on,

"The Queen, who died three years ago, was Hungarian and, I believe, very charming and she did her duty by presenting her husband with two sons."

The Duke saw his daughter shudder and, then realising that he had made a mistake, went on quickly,

"The Crown Prince is married to a woman of German nationality, who the Ambassador tells me no one likes. I am sure, therefore, my dearest, that you will be very popular."

Gloria pressed her lips together to prevent herself from telling her father that she had no wish to be popular in Arginos.

She knew, however, that it would upset him.

So she, therefore, continued to say nothing.

They were in London for only three days when Gloria learned that the Queen wished to meet her.

She was driven in grand style to Windsor Castle with her father.

They made the long journey in a Royal carriage drawn by four fine horses.

As they drew near to Windsor Castle, Gloria enquired,

"I suppose, Papa, we could not have refused to see the Queen?"

"You know as well as I do," the Duke said, "that Her Majesty wants to make sure that you will be a worthy representative of the Union Jack."

He was speaking in a somewhat mocking tone and Gloria could not help exclaiming mischievously,

"Suppose I am not? Will I be discarded – as not good enough for the post?"

The Duke shook his head.

"There is no chance of that. You are very lovely, my precious daughter, and any country would be proud for you to be its representative."

Gloria did not reply to him.

*

Gloria felt overwhelmed when they were ushered into the room where the Queen was waiting for them.

The first thing she noticed was the enormous number of photographs and her father had told her that the Queen always kept them with her. They were packed into her luggage when she moved from place to place.

Then, as Gloria first saw the Queen waiting for them, she seemed in her black gown and white widow's cap to be rather small and insignificant.

As Gloria curtseyed, she became aware that the Queen had a personality and an authority that vibrated from her almost magnetically.

Her Majesty then greeted the Duke.

.Because she had always liked handsome men, she noticed that he had not lost his good looks as he had grown older.

The Queen thought that his face was rather more distinguished-looking than when she had seen him last.

"It is delightful to see Your Grace again," she said to him condescendingly.

"It is a great honour, ma'am, and a great joy to be in Your Majesty's company."

"I cannot think why you have chosen to bury yourself deep in the country!" the Queen said sharply. "I miss you and I would not say that unless it was true."

"I am very honoured, ma'am, that you should remember me," the Duke answered.

"And this is your daughter?" the Queen next asked.

"This is Gloria, my only daughter, whom I shall miss greatly once she is taken from me."

"I understand the girl is over eighteen and it is time she married," the Queen remarked.

She gave Gloria a searching glance before she added,

"I trust you have been sufficiently instructed on exactly how important you will be when you reach the country of Arginos?"

"Indeed, ma'am, it has been all explained to me – in great detail," Gloria answered.

"The Foreign Secretary has in fact talked so much about Arginos," the Duke said, "he thinks it is now blown up out of all proportion to its size."

The Queen gave an unexpected little chuckle.

"To be honest with Your Grace, that is just what I thought myself."

She smiled at the Duke before she said,

"You must persuade your daughter that she must be as efficient in Arginos as you were before you wasted yourself in the country among the cabbages!"

"Your Majesty is more than flattering me," the Duke replied, "but I assure you, ma'am, that they are very delicious cabbages."

The Queen laughed outright.

"You always had an answer to everything, but since you have left the Court, I do not allow people to answer me back!"

She smiled as she held out her hand.

"I suppose as soon as your daughter has left, you will return North to Yorkshire?"

"I am afraid so, ma'am," the Duke answered.

He kissed the Queen's hand and the Queen turned her head to look again at Gloria.

"Now make yourself as efficient as your father," she said, "and always remember that I shall be hearing in detail exactly how you fare in Arginos."

"I will try to carry out – Your Majesty's wishes," Gloria said as she curtseyed again.

She and her father backed slowly from the room.

Only when they were outside did Gloria realise that the interview had not been quite so frightening as she had expected it to be.

They drove back to London, where the Duchess was waiting to hear what had occurred.

"Her Majesty was in a surprisingly good humour," the Duke informed her.

He then told his wife all that had been said and the Duchess sighed with relief.

"If she did not ask after me, she obviously has no wish to see me. I am always afraid that I shall be forced to take up the hereditary post of the Lady-of-the-Bedchamber like the former Duchess of Winton."

"No, you are not wanted at Windsor Castle, thank God!" the Duke said. "And you know I want you with me at home, every day and every minute."

The Duchess smiled at him as he promised her,

"We will go back home as soon as Gloria has left."

*

It was only with superhuman self-control that Gloria managed not to cry when she said 'goodbye' to her beloved father and mother.

A Battleship was waiting for them at Tilbury and there was a distinguished collection of Statesmen and Politicians to see her off.

She knew that this was not only because they were concerned with Arginos, but because her father had not been forgotten even although they seldom saw him.

Everybody paid her effusive compliments.

She also received a number of last-minute instructions that she did not listen to.

Finally the Earl of Derby announced that it was time for the farewell party to go ashore.

Having said her 'goodbyes' to him, the other representatives of the Queen and the Prime Minister, Gloria went below to her cabin.

Her father and mother had accompanied her there and she had been controlled and calm until this moment arrived.

When her mother held out her arms to her, Gloria said,

"If I cannot – bear it, Mama, I shall either come home – or else – throw myself into – the sea!"

"You must not talk like that," the Duchess scolded her, "you know it will distress your father."

"It is not fair – you know it is not fair, that I should have to – go away without you and – marry a man I have – never seen. He may be – cross-eyed and – deaf and dumb for all – I may know!"

"The Ambassador has assured us that he is handsome and very charming. He also said he is an outstanding rider and loves his horses."

Gloria had heard all this before and she did not believe a single word of it.

She kissed her mother and then turned to her father,

"I know why you are not – coming with me – Papa," she said. "It only makes things – worse. But, as I have said to Mama, if everything is – intolerable – I shall come – home."

"I promise you one thing," the Duke said. "If, as you say, it is intolerable, I will come out and stay with you and see what I can do about it."

"You promise? You really – promise?" Gloria asked him.

"I promise," the Duke breathed quietly.

Gloria put her head on his shoulder and now she was fighting against tears.

They held each other close and nobody spoke until they heard a voice in the distance calling out,

"Everyone ashore, if you please!"

"We have to go," the Duke said. "Goodbye, my precious beautiful daughter. I know you will not fail as indeed none of our family has ever failed to serve their country when the need had arisen."

He spoke solemnly and Gloria sensed that it came from his heart.

She had been brought up on the stories of how her ancestors all down the centuries had served England exceedingly well.

"I will – try, Papa," she said in a broken voice.

Her father and mother left her alone in the cabin.

When they had gone, she locked the door and threw herself down on the bed.

She did not cry, because she knew that it was useless.

She only listened to the noise of the engines beneath her and felt the Battleship begin to move slowly away from the quay.

The other members of the party would be out on deck, waving to those who were seeing them off. She, however, had no intention of joining them.

'I am going into exile,' she told herself, 'an exile as empty and miserable as if I was lost in a barren desert. I will be alone – completely alone.'

*

It was some time later when there came a knock on her cabin door.

Gloria thought that it was the Steward, whom she had been told would look after her on the voyage.

She rose to her feet, unlocked the door and found that she had not been mistaken.

"Is there anythin' I can bring you, my Lady?" the Steward asked her. "The fact is, I was thinkin' you might enjoy a glass of champagne. It's what they're drinkin' in the Captain's cabin."

"That is very kind of you," Gloria replied.

The Steward was an elderly man with greying hair and she learned later that he had been aboard the Battleship, which was called *H.M.S. Victorious*, for more than six years.

As he came back with a glass of champagne, he said,

"Now, don't you go about frettin' yourself, my Lady. You'll enjoy seein' Arginos. I've bin there and it's not such a bad place, not bad at all."

Gloria sipped her champagne.

"What – are the – people like?" she managed to ask him.

"They be friendly enough if you can make yourself understood," the Steward replied.

"I have heard that they speak almost pure Greek," Gloria remarked.

She had refused to ask questions about Arginos of those who came to visit The Castle.

Yet now she was prepared to talk about the country with the Steward.

"They'll make a real fuss of you," he said. "Them Greeks has an eye for a pretty woman, and that's somethin' as be missin' at The Palace."

Gloria laughed because she could not help it.

"What do you mean by that?" she asked.

"Well, two years ago, when we were in Port, the King comes aboard. If you asks me, he was just spyin' out what the Battleship were like. The King's actually a decent-looking man. "But you should see the women as comes with him. Plain as the back of a cab, as me old Dad used to say and dressed like somethin' out of the Ark!"

Gloria laughed again.

"Why are they like that?" she asked

"I don't really knows the answer to that," the Steward said. "But they wasn't chosen for their looks, I can tell you that much!"

Gloria took another sip from her glass of champagne.

"And what are the – men of Arginos like?"

She did not mean to ask the question, but, because she was thinking of Prince Darius, she could not help it.

"'Handsome," the Steward answered, "some of them might just be like them Greek Gods they makes so much fuss about."

"That is cheering at any rate," Gloria smiled.

As she had finished her glass, she put it down and the Steward picked it up.

"You'll shine amongst them all right," he said, "and like all them foreigners, they can make a compliment sound as if they were a-givin' you a golden guinea."

He walked towards the door and, as he reached it, he turned back to say,

"What be it the Bible say 'bout a Land of Milk and Honey? That's what your Ladyship'll find in Arginos and you'll enjoy the honey more than the milk!"

He went from the cabin and Gloria found herself laughing once more.

It was the first time she had laughed spontaneously since she had learned that she had to go to Arginos.

Somehow the Steward had broken the ice that seemed to have encased her.

'A Land of Milk and Honey!' she told herself. 'I wonder how true that is? But there will be no honey on my tongue for Prince Darius!'

CHAPTER THREE

If Gloria had not been so worried about what lay ahead of her, she would have enjoyed the voyage a great deal.

It was impossible not to be thrilled about being aboard such a grand British Battleship.

Beside, everybody was doing their best to amuse her.

She found that the Marquis and Marchioness of Garth were charming and the Marquis was particularly interesting to talk to.

She also liked the British Ambassador and his wife, although they were getting old and were rather grumpy.

The Ambassador of Arginos said to her on the morning after they had left England,

"I wonder, Lady Gloria, if you would like to learn a little of our language before you arrive in Arginos?"

For just a moment Gloria wanted to reply that she had no desire to speak to any of the Arginosians, including Prince Darius.

Then she knew that it would be a very undiplomatic and wrong thing for her to say.

She therefore replied,

"Thank you, Your Excellency. I do know Greek quite well because I speak it with Papa and I understand that your language is based on Greek."

"It is indeed," the Ambassador replied. "Suppose you spend two hours with me every morning while I introduce you to Arginos?"

The Duke spoke both Ancient and Modern Greek and had taught them to his sons and his daughter.

Gloria, therefore, found that her lessons with the Ambassador were most enjoyable.

They soon left behind the grammar, which is always boring in any language.

The Ambassador told her, instead, some of the ancient legends of Arginos.

In fact they admired, and perhaps worshipped, the same Gods as the Ancient Greeks.

Gloria was surprised to find that she was very knowledgeable on all the historical tales the Ambassador told her.

Apart from her lessons there were a good number of young and good-looking Officers on board. And they were only too ready to entertain her.

She was taken all over the Battleship, shown how the guns worked and then spent a lot of time on the bridge with the Captain.

It was something that she had never seen before and she found it really fascinating.

As she told herself when she went to bed, the only dark shadow on the horizon was the Prince.

He would be waiting there for her when they finally reached Arginos.

Because she had spent so much time in the country, she was not aware of how much the Officers, the Ship's Company and the other guests admired her.

"She will be a major sensation in Arginos when she arrives," the Marchioness said to her husband.

"I hope so," he replied, "but I have met King Hadrian. He is what I call a rather stuffy man, who is not at all at his ease with young people."

"How do you know that?" the Marchioness laughed.

"I had to pay a Diplomatic visit to the King just after I had been to Constantinople," the Marquis replied, "and I thought it was without exception the dullest time I spent on the whole trip."

The Marchioness gave a little cry.

"Oh, for Goodness' sake, Lionel, don't tell that to this poor child. I know she is suffering at leaving her father and mother whom she adores. It will not make it any easier to marry a stranger if his Palace is what you say it is."

"I have never met Prince Darius," the Marquis said. "As I understand it, he is seldom home. Personally I would not blame him."

What he told his wife made her more attentive towards Gloria than she had been before.

Gloria found herself gradually relaxing and not being so apprehensive of what lay ahead for her.

The sea voyage certainly brought plenty of colour to her cheeks and her hair shone like the sunshine itself as they passed over the smooth waters of the Mediterranean.

Gloria had hoped that they would perhaps stop at Naples and again at Athens.

But the Captain had orders to proceed as quickly as possible to Arginos, although Gloria was not aware of this.

The Marquis knew, however, that the Ambassador was counting the days.

He was afraid that something might happen before the Arginosians knew that they were under the protection of the British flag.

The British Ambassador confirmed to everyone he spoke to that there was every need for haste.

"I have worked in the Balkans," he told the Marquis, "for over ten years now, but I have never known the situation to be as tense as it is at the moment. Although the Foreign Office laughs at my fears, I am quite certain that they are walking a tightrope."

"As bad as that?" the Marquis enquired.

He believed that both Ambassadors were making a 'mountain out of a molehill'.

As he said often to his wife,

"They have little else to excite them and I think that they are unnecessarily apprehensive about Russia swallowing Arginos up."

"I do hope she will not do so until we have visited Constantinople, as you promised me so many times," the Marchioness responded.

"If the Ambassador is to be believed, the Russians may well get there first," the Marquis teased her.

"Well, if they do, I hope they bring some sables with them," the Marchioness said. "That is something you have also promised me!"

The Marquis laughed and kissed her.

He told himself privately, however, that if things seemed at all dangerous, he would take his wife back to England as soon as possible.

He said to the Captain when he went up on the Bridge,

"When you have taken the future bride to Arginos, are you intending to wait for us? Or must we find another ship in which to return to England?"

The Captain thought for a moment and then he said,

"I tell you what I will do, my Lord. When I have dropped you off for the Wedding, I will return to

Athens as I have been told to do. But I will ask if I can come back and pick you up before we move into the Mediterranean, where I have, on the Admiral's instructions, to meet with several other Battleships."

"That is very kind of you," the Marquis replied. "We would much rather travel with you than return to England in any other ship and least of all by train."

"I am told that is a very perilous journey," the Captain commented smiling.

"So I believe," the Marquis said. "Personally I detest trains and find them unsettling."

The days at sea passed quickly.

Finally Gloria had to face the fact that tomorrow she would arrive at Koloni, which was the Capital of Arginos.

They all dined in the Captain's cabin on the last night of the voyage and he proposed a toast to her health and everybody wished her the best of luck.

'It is what I shall – need,' Gloria thought to herself.

Aloud she now said,

"Thank you all very much. It is difficult for me to tell you how much I have enjoyed this voyage. I only wish that my father and mother could have been with me."

There was a wistful note in her voice and an expression in her eyes that made every man present, young or old, want to comfort and protect her.

She looked very small and very fragile.

Even the women present were thinking it was cruel that she had to go alone to a strange country and marry a man she had never even met.

The British Ambassadress, as if it was her duty, escorted Gloria to her cabin later in the evening.

"You know, Lady Gloria," she said in her rather prim voice, "that, if my husband or I can do anything for you that will help, it will be a pleasure and you have only to ask for what you want."

'Thank you," Gloria replied. "It is very kind of you to say that."

"I really do mean it," the Ambassadress pointed out, "and, although we have never met Prince Darius, I am sure he is a very charming young man."

Gloria stared at her in surprise.

"You have never met him?" she asked. "But your husband said you have been in Arginos for some years."

"The Prince has always been away," the Ambassadress replied. "In fact I have seen him only once or twice on formal occasions, but have never actually been introduced to him."

Gloria thought it was very extraordinary and so she asked,

"Why is he away from the country so much? Where does he go?"

"I do not really know," the Ambassadress answered. "As he is the younger son, he had not been of much importance to my husband, who deals directly either with His Majesty or else the Crown Prince."

There was obviously no point in asking her any more, but Gloria thought it was rather strange.

Late that night, because she could not sleep, she was aware that the engines had almost stopped.

The Battleship was still out at sea and then she understood that they were waiting until morning before they moved into Port.

There, a deputation would be waiting to greet her to their country.

Finding it hard to sleep, her hatred for the Prince came back even stronger than before.

She wished that she could turn the Battleship round and take her back to England.

*

When she was called in the morning, she was aware from the throb of the engines that the *Victorious* was moving slowly.

"What time are we expected to arrive?" she asked the Steward.

"Sharp on noon, my Lady," he replied, "not a minute earlier, nor a minute later. Them be our orders."

He brought her breakfast in bed.

She thought it was tactful of him to understand, without her saying so, that she wanted to eat her breakfast alone.

She had no wish to chatter about her arrival with all the other guests on board.

"Now, you eat a good breakfast, my Lady," the Steward said. "Your will need all your strength to cope with all that cheerin' and flag-wavin' and I expects, whether you wants it or not, there'll be long speeches from men as would make the story of the Battle of Waterloo sound dreary!"

Gloria laughed as he meant her to do.

She thought that no one else could have made her feel so light-hearted at such a moment.

When she had dressed, she put on the gown that her mother had chosen for her to wear on her arrival.

"First impressions are always important, my dearest," the Duchess had said, "as that is the way they will always remember you after the cheering has stopped."

"You are quite certain that there will be some," Gloria remarked.

"Of course there will be," the Duchess remarked. "I am sure everybody in the country has been told that you are the lifeline that is going to save them. No one, however stupid they may be, wants to be conquered by another hostile country."

"I do hope you are right, Mama," Gloria had replied.

Her gown was certainly spectacular. In fact it was so pretty that she thought the women of the country would undoubtedly admire her.

It had been made on Bond Street in London and was of a very pale pink, the colour of a musk rose.

It accentuated her figure at the front and behind and there was an attractive small bustle.

The hat that went with it was turned back from her face so that she could be seen by the crowd.

It was massed with roses and some of them were tucked underneath the brim over her left ear.

She went up on deck, because the Battleship was moving even more slowly into Port.

When the Marchioness saw her, she exclaimed,

"Oh, you do look so pretty. I am sure that your mother must have chosen this gown for you."

"She did," Gloria replied. "I would certainly hope that the people of Arginos will like it as well."

"They will love it," the Marchioness assured her.

The two Ambassadresses said almost exactly the same thing.

There was no need for the men, neither those who travelled with her or served aboard, to express what they felt in words.

Without being in the least conceited, Gloria could easily see the admiration in their eyes.

She would like to have gone out on deck to see the Battleship move alongside the quay.

She had been informed by the Captain that there was a large crowd waiting to greet her.

The Ambassadress thought it would be a mistake for her to appear until the last moment.

"I expect Prince Darius will come on board first," she said. "Then the Prime Minister and the other Statesmen. When they have welcomed you to the country, there will be speeches on the quayside so that the crowds can hear the speakers and cheer loudly at all that they have to say."

Gloria did not reply.

She was feeling once again frightened and at the same time angry.

Her heart was a hard stone in her breast.

She knew that she would have to be very careful to keep her self-control and no one must realise how much she resented being forced into a Diplomatic marriage.

It was, she told herself forcefully, completely inhuman.

The Battleship came alongside the quay and then the party that had come from England all gathered on the upper deck.

Because it was now hot an awning had been spread several days previously.

Once beneath it, it was impossible for those standing on the quay to see them.

Gloria, however, could see that there was a great deal of bunting and flags and quite a few Union Jacks.

A man appeared and he was escorted by the Captain of the Battleship.

He was wearing a white uniform coat, heavily bestrewn with decorations.

Gloria drew in her breath.

She found it hard to look at him.

Now she would see Prince Darius for the first time.

The Ambassador who was standing beside her said in a low voice,

"It is the Crown Prince, who has come to welcome you."

Gloria looked at him and saw that he was in fact older than she had expected Prince Darius to be.

He was a rather dull-looking man wearing spectacles.

He advanced towards her.

As she curtseyed, he started to speak in a slow rather monotonous tone of voice,

"May I welcome you, Lady Gloria, to my country and tell you just how exceedingly glad we are to see you and how grateful to Her Majesty Queen Victoria for sending you to us in our hour of need."

He spoke in English, which was actually quite good, although he mispronounced one or two words slightly.

There were also pauses while he was thinking out what he had to say next.

He then greeted the rest of the English party, speaking again in English to the Marquis and Marchioness and to the British Ambassador.

After that, with an obvious sigh of relief, he spoke in his own language.

The Captain had provided glasses of champagne for this informal meeting.

Gloria refused, thinking that she should keep her brain clear for what would come next.

As she had been warned, there were long speeches once they had left the Battleship.

The Crown Prince had a great deal to say about his country and the Prime Minister was even more long-winded.

It was a great relief when they could get into the open carriages that were to carry them to The Palace.

Gloria sat beside the Crown Prince in the first one and there was only an Equerry sitting opposite them.

The others followed behind.

As they drove off, Gloria was aware that the carriages were old and in need of a good polishing as well as extensive repairs.

The horses, while white as was usual on such occasions, had also passed the best years of their lives.

She forced herself, however, to be more concerned about the people who were lining the streets, waving to her as she passed them.

Some of them wore their native dress, which was much the same as that worn by other countries of the Balkans.

The majority, however, seemed to be poorly garbed and the houses on either side of the route were not particularly impressive.

She then wondered to herself if the country was indeed as poor as it appeared. It was a question that she had not asked before she left England.

If it was, she thought uncomfortably, her elegant and really expensive gowns would be singularly out of place.

There was no doubt that the crowds were pleased to see her.

Some of the mothers held up their children.

She wondered if they wanted to impress her or the children themselves. She noticed that a great number of them carried a small Union flag.

The Palace was at the far end of the Capital City.

The ground rose higher as they progressed until Gloria realised that The Palace was built on the top of a hill.

There was a profusion of trees encircling it and protecting it at the back.

It was not, however, all that spectacular.

She was disappointed that it was not a white Palace, which she knew that a lot of other countries could boast about.

The horses climbed slowly towards some steps leading up to what Gloria imagined was the main entrance.

Almost as if he understood the question that she had not asked, the Crown Prince said,

"We do not use this entrance except on formal occasions and this, of course, is surely a very important one."

"W-who will be – waiting for me?" Gloria asked him rather nervously.

"My father, the King," the Crown Prince replied, "my wife and, I hope – my brother."

As there was a distinct pause before the last two words, Gloria could not help saying,

"The Ambassador told me that Prince Darius would meet me on the Battleship. It was very kind of you to come in his place."

"It is what my brother should have done," the Crown Prince muttered. "And my father had arranged that I should meet you with him when you reached The Palace."

He spoke in an exasperated tone. Because he was obviously annoyed with his brother, it made him a little more human than he had seemed up until now.

He was certainly stiff and pedantic and Gloria wondered if it was because he was shy of her or perhaps he was habitually rather cold and distant to everyone he met.

If that was the truth, and the rest of the family was just like him, it would be even worse living in The Palace than she had anticipated.

The carriage came to a stop and footmen in white wigs opened the door.

Gloria thought that their Livery and their wigs were slightly shabby.

However, she did not want to be critical so soon after her arrival.

She forced herself to try not to notice that the red carpet that the steps were covered with was definitely threadbare.

Soldiers lined the steps on either side.

Their uniform was certainly different in many ways from that of any British Regiment.

She and the Crown Prince walked up the steps first.

When they reached the top, the doors were opened.

As they walked through them, Gloria found herself in a large hall.

She was facing a company of people in the centre of which, it was easy to recognise the King. He was wearing such a profusion of jewelled decorations that his whole tunic sparkled with them.

There was a blue and yellow ribbon across his chest and it was the identical way that her father wore the Order of the Garter.

The moment that Gloria appeared, there was a fanfare of trumpets.

As she rose from a deep curtsey and the sound died away, the King, speaking in his own language, began,

"Welcome to Arginos. I sincerely hope that you will be very happy with us, my Lady."

He then went into a long eulogy about Queen Victoria that Gloria had already heard from the Crown Prince and the Prime Minister.

She listened to it all as attentively as she could manage.

When the King finished, she was introduced to the Statesmen and the members of the Royal Household who were grouped round him.

She met the wife of the Crown Prince and a number of elderly men and women who she gathered were close relatives of the King.

The whole Cabinet was there with their wives as were the Heads of the Army and the Navy.

Only when she finished shaking hands did she then realise that there was still no sign of Prince Darius.

Then there was a procession led by the King, with Gloria at his side, towards the dining room.

It was a large room and ten long tables were required to seat all the guests present.

The walls were dark and the ceiling seemed to be the same until Gloria realised that they were really discoloured with age.

The curtains on either side of the windows were also of heavy red velvet and had lost their lustre.

She became more acutely aware that at the top of the head table there was an empty chair.

It should have been, she thought, next to hers.

The Crown Prince, however, after an obvious delay, then sat down next to her.

She, therefore, had the King on her left hand side and him on her right.

She would have been very foolish if she had not been aware that the non-appearance of Prince Darius had annoyed and agitated his family.

The whispered remarks between them that she understood because she could now speak their language pretty well all concerned him.

The King was frowning and it suddenly struck Gloria as being particularly funny.

She had been apprehensive and afraid of meeting the Prince.

It was now quite obvious that he felt very much the same about her.

He had, therefore, disappeared.

She could hear the King muttering about it to the Crown Princess, who was sitting on his other side.

She knew too that the Crown Prince kept looking towards the door as if he expected his brother to appear at any moment.

'If he really cannot be found,' Gloria said to herself, 'then I will be able to leave here and go home.'

She felt her spirits rise at the idea.

Then she was quite sure that, having brought her to his country, the King would not let her leave.

He was older than she had expected him to be and almost bald.

What hair he had was dead white and, like the Crown Prince, he wore spectacles and they did seem to fit him very well.

Only because of his many resplendent decorations could he in any way be considered an impressive figure.

She had the idea that most of the Courtiers and Statesmen present were in awe of him.

They also seemed very old and somewhat dilapidated.

When she looked round, she remembered what the Steward had said about the plainness of the Arginos women.

There were only one or two young faces to be seen in the whole room.

The majority of those, who appeared to be the wives of Statesmen, were definitely plain and uninspiring.

The relatives who she had met first on her arrival were certainly well all over forty.

'Everybody in this country cannot be old,' she told herself. 'There must be some young and exciting locals somewhere, but certainly those of high standing are all elderly.'

Apart from the King and the Crown Prince, she thought that amongst the Statesmen were some who looked Greek.

But they too were undoubtedly getting on in years and they might well have been very handsome when they were young and agile.

Yet there were none of the 'Apollos' or other Greek Gods that she had been expecting to see in Arginos.

It suddenly occurred to her that she might have to spend the rest of her life talking to the old and aged.

She would in consequence feel very young and perhaps appear to be somewhat ignorant in their presence.

The food was good and nourishing, but not particularly imaginative. And then the wine, of which Gloria took only a sip or two, was definitely insipid.

"Have you any vineyards in Arginos?" she asked the Crown Prince.

"I don't think so," he replied. "I suppose we could grow grapes, but it is something we have not tried to do in the past. Our wine is all imported and mostly from Croatia."

The luncheon dragged on for ever and ever it seemed to Gloria.

When she was hoping that it would soon come to an end, one Statesman after another asked to say 'a few words.'

Everything they said was very much the same as had been said before them.

They welcomed Gloria to their country because she represented the Queen of England and they claimed that there was no greater or more powerful group of countries in the whole world than the British Empire.

It was quite obvious that they were cheering each other up and trying to disperse their fear of the Russians without actually saying so.

So they spoke in a dull and rather muddled manner.

Gloria began to believe that the meal would never come to an end.

At last, however, the King rose to his feet and everyone stopped talking.

With Gloria walking beside him, they moved from the room, the guests curtseying and bowing as they passed.

Only when they had left and were in the corridor outside did Gloria hear everyone begin to talk again.

And it was in a far more animated tone than she had heard before.

The King took her into a large drawing room that seemed a little more cheerful than the dull dining room.

There was very little colour, except from the sunshine streaming in through the windows.

"I expect," the King turned to Gloria, "that you would now like to see your rooms. But I thought first that you would wish to say 'goodbye' to your companions on *H.M.S. Victorious*, who will now be leaving us."

Gloria looked surprised.

"Do you mean that the Marquis and Marchioness are not staying here in The Palace?"

"No, they are staying at the British Embassy," the King said. "I find it a nuisance to have too many guests and I already have a large number of relatives who insisted on coming to meet you."

Gloria wanted to protest that she would very much like at least one or two English ladies and gentlemen to be near her at The Palace.

Then she thought that, if the King then refused her, it would be uncomfortable.

At the first opportunity she said quietly to the Marchioness,

"I thought you would be staying here with me."

"I thought so too," the Marchioness replied, "but we are coming back for dinner and, of course, I will come and see you tomorrow. I am afraid, however, that you will have a great number of deputations, which will leave you with very little time to yourself."

"Please come and tell me what is happening," Gloria pleaded.

"I will, of course," the Marchioness replied, "although I am sure that there will be an *aide-de-camp* who will have a special programme for you. I doubt if you will have a second to yourself before your marriage actually takes place."

She was speaking lightly as if she meant to cheer up Gloria, who, however, asked,

"When am I to be married? Nobody has told me."

"It has been arranged for three days from now," the Marchioness replied.

"Three days!" Gloria exclaimed. "But I have not even met Prince Darius yet!"

The Marchioness hesitated.

Before she could say anything more, the Crown Prince joined them.

"I must apologise," he said to the Marchioness, "and, of course, to you, Lady Gloria, but my brother was slightly indisposed this morning and that was why he was unable to appear either when you arrived or at the luncheon party."

"I hope it is nothing serious," the Marchioness queried.

"Oh, no, no!" the Crown Prince answered. "I am sure he will be well enough to dine with us tonight."

"Are we coming to dinner at The Palace?" the Marchioness asked.

"Of course you are," the Crown Prince replied. "My father is eager to talk to you and to your husband. It is just that we have so many relations with us that there is hardly a room left unoccupied."

Gloria knew that this was untrue because of the way that he hesitated over what he was saying.

She thought it extremely tiresome of the King to make the Marquis and the Marchioness go to the British Embassy. They were, after all, looking after her on behalf of Her Majesty the Queen.

"Please, when you come back tonight, make it quite clear that you want to be with me tomorrow," she said to the Marchioness.

"I think you will have to do that," the Marchioness replied. "It is certainly very unusual for this to happen."

One of the King's relatives asked Gloria if she could take her upstairs to her bedroom.

The staircase was very impressive.

The walls were again dark, either panelled or painted in shades of brown both in the hall and along the corridors.

There were, however, only a few pictures that looked attractive.

There were also pieces of furniture which Gloria was sure were centuries old and very valuable.

When she reached her bedroom, it was as disappointing as the rest of The Palace.

There was nothing bright or cheerful about it.

The bed was carved, but it had not been gilded as it would have been in England.

The covers and curtains, both on the bed and the windows, were of a deep velvet.

In some lights they appeared to be a ruby red and in others a dull brown.

The whole impression of the room was gloomy.

The relative who had been chattering as they came up the stairs was obviously impressed by it.

"This has always been one of the most outstanding rooms in The Palace," she said, "but, of course, the King's Suite is the most magnificent."

"Do the Crown Prince and his wife also live in The Palace or do they have a house of their own?" Gloria asked.

"His Royal Highness has been petitioning the King for some years to be allowed to move into a smaller Palace. I think he is going to try even harder for his father's permission now that you are here."

"Then my husband and I will also live in The Palace?" Gloria wanted to know.

"Yes, of course," the relative answered. "If the Crown Prince cannot have a house to himself, there is no chance of a younger son having one."

She spoke as if she thought that Gloria was expecting far too much and it was in fact somewhat impertinent of her.

Gloria lifted her chin.

"In England," she said, "most young couples want to be alone and not be overshadowed by their relatives."

There was an uncomfortable pause.

Then the Princess, whom Gloria was to learn later was the younger sister of the King, said,

"Our ways are very different from your ways and you will find when you have lived here for some time that we do not like change.

"The Kings of Arginos have always had their close family around them. That is why my brother dislikes the idea of breaking this tradition, which, I can assure you, my dear, is always a mistake."

With great difficulty, Gloria prevented herself from saying what she wanted to say.

Only when the Princess had left her and she was alone did she take off her hat and throw it onto the bed.

She then started to explore what rooms had been allotted to her as the bride of a younger son.

She found that there was a boudoir opening out of her bedroom.

Because it was large, she might even call it a drawing room.

It might be very large, but it was also very gloomy.

Beyond it was a dining room, large enough to seat twelve people with some comfort and, opening out of it, there was a pantry.

Gloria turned back to leave her bedroom by a door on the other side.

Here there was a large closet to hold her clothes and at the end of the passage that led from her bedroom there was a door.

She was sure without being told that it would be to the Prince's bedroom.

There seemed to be no sign of anybody joining her.

Because she was curious, she put out her hand to touch the handle of the door.

If there was nobody there, she would just peep in to see what the room was like. Also she wanted to be certain that she was not wrong in her assumption that it belonged to the Prince.

However, when she turned the handle, she found that the door was locked.

She turned to go back into her own room.

As she did so, two maids came hurrying in, obviously flustered.

They curtseyed and explained volubly that they had not been told she had come upstairs.

The luggage was just being brought up by the footmen.

It had arrived from the Battleship after some delay because of the large crowds.

The maids talked at a great speed.

Gloria was, however, delighted to find that she could understand everything that they were saying to her

The King and his family were slow talkers and their tones monotonous.

These maids were definitely very different.

They expressed themselves strangely eloquently, using their hands as if gestures were more important than words.

Gloria assured them that she was not in the least upset that she had been alone.

When the luggage arrived, it was taken into the closet.

Having tidied her hair in the mirror, Gloria then walked into the sitting room.

Now, as she looked at it again, she thought that it was definitely exceedingly ugly.

'How can I live with this?' she asked herself. '*How can I?*'

Even as she asked the question, the door opened.

A man appeared and she looked at him questioningly.

He stared at her.

She knew, even before he spoke a word, that this was Prince Darius, who was alleged to be indisposed.

He stood looking at her and she saw that he was very different from his brother. For one thing he was taller and his hair was dark.

He had definite clean-cut Grecian features together with a long moustache and his figure was clearly very athletic.

He looked at her in a somewhat penetrating manner, as if he was inspecting her minutely.

He seemed to be looking 'beneath the surface', although she had no idea of how he could do so.

He closed the door behind him.

Then, as she just stood gazing at him, he said in English,

"I suppose I should apologise for not meeting you as you had expected."

"I was told that you were ill," Gloria replied.

"I was not ill," the Prince replied, "but merely sick at the idea of being pressured into marriage. In fact, to be frank with you, I loathe the whole idea."

Gloria felt her temper rising.

"If that is your attitude. Your Royal Highness," she said, "perhaps you would like to hear mine. I was appalled when I was told that I had to marry you when I had not even seen you. I had no wish to come here and, if you want the truth, I hate you and the whole idea of having to be married to you!"

CHAPTER FOUR

As she finished speaking, Gloria realised that she had been extremely rude.

She was still flushed with anger at her dislike for the Prince.

After a pregnant pause of several minutes he said,

"At least you are frank!"

"I see no point in being anything else," Gloria replied. "I have come here merely because I do not want Her Majesty the Queen Victotia to vent her wrath on my family."

"I have always heard that she is a ferocious despot," the Prince commented.

He walked across the room to stand in front of the fireplace.

Gloria thought that it was what her father always did when he was thinking.

She was sure that the Prince was disconcerted by her behaviour, but it did not trouble her in any way.

She merely thought that it was good for him to know the whole truth about her situation as soon as possible

What was more, she had no intention of being imposed upon by him or anyone else.

After a few seconds the Prince said,

"I suppose you have been told that I am a traveller and I am seldom here in my father's Kingdom?"

"Somebody did mention it," Gloria replied. "I think you are very lucky to be able to go to the places in the world which I have only been able to read about in books and magazines."

"It has certainly been more than interesting," the Prince said, "and something I would very much wish to continue doing."

He said the last words positively and Gloria then asked him,

"Are you implying that when we are married you will go away and then leave me here alone?"

"That is certainly my idea," the Prince nodded.

Once again Gloria felt her temper rising.

"And what do you think I will be doing while you will be away enjoying yourself in other countries?"

The Prince made a gesture with his hands.

"What all women do in the same circumstances," he replied, " – gossip, shop and have children."

"I thought that was what you would say eventually," Gloria remarked.

She forced herself to speak quietly as she said in a very positive manner,

"I decided to tell you when we met that I have no intention of being a complacent wife and, most of all,

I would not allow any man whom I did not love to touch me."

The Prince looked at her in surprise.

"Love?" he replied. "Do you really believe that love can come into a marriage arranged for Royal families?"

"My mother, in order to marry my father – because she loved him, renounced her title," Gloria said. "All my life I have lived with two people who are overwhelmingly in love with each other."

She paused and, as the Prince did not speak, she went on,

"I cannot imagine anything more unpleasant than having a child by a man I do not love and – who does not love me."

She spoke the last words as if they were a challenge and then there was a sudden silence.

She realised that the Prince was thinking and finally he said,

"I suppose as my brother is Heir to the Throne and although he has only daughters, there is no reason why he should not have a son. It is, therefore, not really necessary that I should contribute to the population."

He spoke slowly as if he was thinking it all out carefully.

Gloria made a sound that was one of joy.

"Do you mean that?" she asked. "Do you really mean it?"

"I cannot see that the old fuddy-duddies who are forcing us into marriage can make us have children if we have no wish to do so," he said at length.

"That makes things so much easier for me," Gloria answered. "I was afraid of meeting you simply because I thought that you would not listen to me."

"You are certainly a surprise," the Prince admitted, "and not the least what I expected an Englishwoman to look like."

Gloria smiled.

"I resemble my mother, who came from Lichenberg."

"I have heard that," the Prince said, "and I admire her for being brave enough to marry your father in the face of opposition from her family."

"They are and were very very happy," Gloria emphasised in a soft voice.

"And that is what you hoped to be too," the Prince said.

"Of course," she agreed, "and I could not believe that I would not only be forced to marry you – a man I had not seen – but brought here in what I consider is indecent haste!"

The Prince smiled.

"You are making me feel sorry for you, which I had no idea of being when I came into the room."

"I thought it was somewhat strange that you did not meet me when I arrived at the Port."

"They made such a fuss about it that they almost brought me to the quay in chains. So I was determined that I would not obey them."

"I should have thought that was a Revolution – in itself!"

"It is, as far as those old fools are concerned," the Prince replied.

"Who are you talking about?" Gloria asked. "The Prime Minister? The Cabinet?"

"Yes, all of them, including my father," the Prince replied. "The only time we have ever taken positive action or done anything that I think would help the country, is in bringing you here. And for that I had to be the sacrificial lamb."

The way he said it seemed so funny that Gloria laughed.

It was something she had not expected to do with the Prince under any circumstances.

"If I am not what you expected," she said, "you are certainly very different from what I thought you would be."

"What did you expect?" he asked curiously.

"Someone, I suppose, like your brother – very conventional."

"And a crashing bore!" the Prince added. "I can see you are intelligent, so you must have found him just as much of a bore as I do. And his wife is worse."

Gloria held up her hands in supposed horror.

"I am sure we ought not to talk like that, not immediately after I have just arrived."

"We are speaking the truth," the Prince said. "Unless you are blind, deaf and dumb, you must be aware that Arginos takes the prize for being the most boring Kingdom in the whole of the Balkans and, as far as I am concerned, in the whole wide world."

"Then why do you not do something about it?" Gloria asked.

The Prince spread out his hands.

"What can I do?" he asked. "Any suggestion I make is ignored because I am the younger son. Every time I speak I am told to shut up. It has been drummed into me ever since I was in the nursery that I am of no particular consequence."

"Until now," Gloria said.

"You are quite right," the Prince agreed, "until now."

"So you might be able to change things," she suggested.

"I might also try to tip over Mount Vesuvius! There is not a man in the Government who would not oppose any suggestion of change or any improvement to anything."

"Can that really be true?" Gloria asked.

"Unfortunately my father is quite determined that everything in this country should be as it was fifty or a hundred years ago. None of the new improvements or inventions that are now quite commonplace in Europe have reached Arginos. It is rather like living on the Ark, as you will find after you have been here a little time."

"And yet you agreed to do something original in saying that you would marry the Union Jack?"

The Prince laughed.

"Is that what you call yourself?"

"It is what I have been told that I am by the Queen, by the Secretary of State for Foreign Affairs, by my father and *'Uncle Tom Cobley and All'*."

The Prince laughed again spontaneously.

He walked from the mantelpiece to sit down on the sofa beside Gloria.

"It seems odd to say it," he said, "but I like you and, now that I think of it, feeling as you do, I consider it very brave of you to come here."

"Like you I had no alternative," Gloria said, "but I hated you the moment I was told your name and all the time I was coming through the Mediterranean and up the Aegean Sea."

"Now you are frightening me," the Prince said. "If you are a witch, I shall expect terrible things to happen to me as a result of your curses."

"I will turn them off," Gloria said, "if you will promise me one thing."

"What is it?" Prince Darius asked her warily.

'That you will be honest with me and also tell me just what you are doing. I am rather nervous in case I will wake up one morning to find that you have vanished on one of your travels and no one knows where you have gone."

"It was certainly something that was in my mind," the Prince confessed.

"I thought I was right in thinking of it," Gloria remarked.

"Don't tell me you are a mind-reader as well as being a witch!" he said. "I am becoming nervous."

"I have been nervous – in fact very frightened," Gloria admitted.

She spoke in a low tone and with a sincerity that the Prince did not miss.

"I am sorry about that," he said, "but then I expected you to be a senseless hearty young Englishwoman who would be too proud and too arrogant to admit that she was frightened, even if she was."

"Well, I was indeed very frightened at the thought of coming here and meeting you," she said. "But now I have seen your relatives, your Politicians and your father, I am frightened of being left alone with them and having absolutely no one to talk to."

The Prince looked away from her.

"What you are really saying," he said after what seemed a long pause, "is that if I go off on my travels, you do not wish to be left behind."

Gloria's eyes lit up.

"Will you take me with you?" she queried. "It would be so wonderful for me. I promise you I will be very good and do exactly what you tell me to do."

"That is a very big promise," the Prince said. "I will certainly consider it."

"And you will – not run away – without telling me?" Gloria pleaded.

He turned to look at her.

Now she thought that there was a different expression in his eyes than there had been before.

"How on earth, looking as you do and speaking as you do, did you get yourself involved in this mess?" he asked.

"That is easy," Gloria said. "I was the only relative of Queen Victoria's left unmarried."

"'The Matchmaker of Europe'," the Prince said. "I have heard her called that in every country."

"The Foreign Secretary told me that there were no less than twenty-three of her blood on Royal Thrones and, although I am only half-Royal because of my Mama, I have to obey the Queen's orders, which are to marry you and help your country."

The Prince made no comment and after a moment Gloria then asked,

"Are things really as bad as they have been – made out to be? Are the Russians *really* making serious trouble – in your country?"

"Of course they are," the Prince answered. "I have warned my father for at least three years now of what they were doing and plotting."

"And what have your people done about it?"

"Absolutely nothing!" the Prince said angrily. "They have not increased the Army, nor have they bought any new weapons. They are still using old-fashioned cannon, which should have been disposed of years ago."

Gloria stared at him in disbelief.

"It seems to be so extraordinary! Surely your father has better advisors than those old men who made speeches when I arrived?"

"It is all that they ever do," the Prince said. "Make speeches and say that everything is perfect even when it is not and tell me that I am such a fool when I say that the Army should be increased in numbers and brought up to date.

"And the same applies to the Navy. At the moment we have one Battleship, which is so small you can hardly see it!"

"They just cannot believe that it is only me who will be able to keep the Russians from behaving badly?"

"It may make them a little more cautious than they have been in the last six months," the Prince replied, "but personally I very much doubt it!"

Gloria was quiet for a moment.

Then she said,

"The Earl of Derby, who is our Secretary of State for Foreign Affairs, is quite convinced that the Russians are afraid of upsetting – Great Britain."

"Then he is being very optimistic," the Prince said. "I only wish that I was."

Gloria clasped her fingers together.

"What can we do about it?" she asked.

The Prince raised his eyebrows.

"Are you really suggesting that *we* should do something together?"

"You can hardly allow the Russians to take over your country unopposed," Gloria said.

The Prince stared at her.

"You really are a most extraordinary girl," he said. "I have told my father over and over again that I wash my hands of the whole thing. He will not listen to me when I bring him positive proof of what the Russians are doing underground. He 'pooh-poohs' it and listens to our Ministers of State who, just like ostriches, bury their heads in the sand and pretend that nothing untoward is happening."

"I think that you should do more than you have done already," Gloria said positively.

She was arguing with the Prince in exactly the same way that she talked over political situations in detail with her father.

"And what do you suggest I do?" the Prince asked. "I have told you that the Cabinet will not listen to me and the Head of the Army is the biggest fool that ever walked the earth."

Gloria thought for a moment.

Then she said,

"If they will not listen to you, then you must talk to the people themselves."

The Prince raised his eyebrows.

"Are you suggesting that I lead a Revolution against my father and his Government?"

"If the situation is as dangerous as you fear, then your country comes first and, as you are an Arginosian, you cannot want to lose it."

The Prince rose and walked to the window. He stood with his back to her and Gloria knew that he was thinking over what she had just said.

She had spoken to him spontaneously, but it was almost as if the words had been put into her mouth.

She realised, although she was not quite certain how, that for him to run away was no answer to the problem.

The Prince turned back to face her.

"You have certainly made me think," he said. "All I can say is that, if there is going to be a Revolution in The Palace, it will be you who has caused it!"

Gloria laughed.

"Now you are offering me a challenge while I thought that I was offering you one."

"As you have already suggested," the Prince replied, *"we* may have to solve it together."

"That will take some time," Gloria said. "I suppose you realise that we are being married in three days' time?"

"It was being drummed into my head every second of last week," the Prince answered her.

Gloria looked at him curiously.

"Why only last week?" she asked.

"Because I was abroad and no one knew where I was. I came home because I had run out of money!"

Gloria made an exclamation of surprise.

"Are you telling me that it was only a week ago that you knew you had to marry me?"

"It was all arranged behind my back and you can well imagine that, if it came to you as a shock, so it did to me!"

"How can they do such things to us?" Gloria asked. "It is totally – uncivilised."

"That is exactly what I thought," the Prince agreed. "When they told me that you were on the way and everything had been arranged, I had no alternative but to agree."

"So, of course, you had to," Gloria said. "The Queen would have been furious if I had arrived only to be sent back labelled 'unwanted'!"

The Prince laughed.

"Can you imagine the turmoil it would have caused, but it would have been worth doing something as outrageous as that just to see their faces?"

Gloria laughed too.

"I am surprised that you did not disappear as soon as you found out what was waiting for you here."

"I thought of it," the Prince said honestly, "but then, as you would have said, I thought of my country and knew that Arginos, small as it is, could not take on the whole of the British Empire single-handedly."

Gloria laughed again.

"I think perhaps you were rather 'chickenhearted', but here I am and, whether you like it or not – we are to be married."

"Shall I say," the Prince asked, "that it does not seem such a terrifying proposition as it did before I came into this room."

"And I am not – so frightened," Gloria admitted. "At the same time you will remember your – promise?"

"I will remember it," the Prince agreed, "and I will try to behave myself a little better than I have up until this moment."

"That is certainly a step in the right direction." Gloria smiled.

"Now you are talking like Queen Victoria," the Prince complained. "If you think I am going to behave like Prince Albert and then walk three steps behind you, you are very much mistaken!"

Gloria gave a little chuckle.

"You have forgotten – that is my position," she replied. "I am only half-Royal and I am quite certain your sister-in-law, if no one else, will never let me forget it."

"If you grow like her," the Prince said, "I shall strangle you! I have never got on very well with my brother, who is an awful 'stick in the mud'. At the same time I feel desperately sorry for him being married to a woman like that!"

Gloria giggled because she could not help it.

"Now we are being unkind," she said, "and you know as well as I do that it would be very wrong and unladylike, to criticise those who are soon to be my relations until I have come to know them better."

"All I can say is that when you do, you will find that they are in fact much worse than they seem now," the Prince said.

He glanced at the clock.

"I suppose I had better go and dress for dinner. I have no wish to sit through two hours of utter boredom, but it is what we are both expected to do."

"I had better dress too," Gloria said, "and I hope, when you see it, you will admire my gown. I feel no one else will, as they do not seem to have kept up with the latest fashions in this part of the world."

"I told you, they have all come out of the Ark," the Prince said, "and Noah, or whoever brought them here, kept all the best-looking clothes for himself."

Gloria giggled again.

"You are being very unkind," she said. "I fully admit that I do feel that I have very little in common with the Ladies of the Court."

"I have been avoiding them for years," the Prince said. "And it is what I shall continue to do for the rest of my life."

He was speaking jokingly, but Gloria then asked him,

"Do we really have to live here in The Palace when we are married?"

The Prince stared at her.

"Are you suggesting that we should do anything else?"

"If we were in England, we would have a house of our own, however small, but the Princess told me that it was impossible and we had to live with the rest of the family."

"When I realised a week ago that I was to be married," the Prince said, "this situation had not crossed my mind. But I will certainly try to do something about it, although it will not be easy."

"Why not?" Gloria enquired.

"Because I am entirely dependent on my father."

"You mean he would not give you money to live anywhere except in The Palace."

"I am quite certain he would refuse point blank," the Prince said. "I suppose you have no money of your own?"

"I have some," Gloria admitted. "But I doubt if it will be enough. My father gave me an allowance last year when I became eighteen. I believe I did have something extra in the way of a Marriage Settlement, which is currently being arranged by the Marquis of Garth with the Arginosian Ambassador."

"My father is a very rich man," the Prince said. "However, like all autocrats, he is very generous when he wants to be, but a miser otherwise."

"Then what can we do?" Gloria asked.

"Leave it to me," the Prince said. "I will fix up something. I have never wanted to live in The Palace and I am sure that we can find a house outside the City where at least we shall be on our own."

"Please do that," Gloria insisted.

The Prince looked at her critically.

"Are you really saying that you want to be with me?"

"It is 'Hobson's Choice," Gloria replied, "and, if I have to choose between you and The Palace, then you will certainly get my vote."

The Prince threw back his head and laughed.

"You are incorrigible. I see that my marriage is to be very different from what I might have expected."

"I should hope so, considering you wanted to opt out of it and disappear into the wilds," Gloria remarked. "And even if you do, I would rather be left alone in a house of my own than cramped here with your large number of relatives penning me in."

"That is exactly the right word," the Prince approved, "and what I already find myself."

He walked towards the door.

"Now leave it to me," he said. "Of course, not a word to anyone, otherwise I can assure you it will be 'nipped in the bud' before such an outrageous idea is even whispered about."

"I will be very careful," she promised, "and naturally on my best behaviour at dinner."

She gave him a smile as she walked towards the door which led into her bedroom.

She heard the Prince leave the sitting room.

Only as the door closed did she think that the interview had been even stranger than she could have imagined.

She knew that in her inner self she was now not quite so nervous or frightened as she had been previously.

*

Dinner, as the Prince had warned Gloria, was a long drawn-out and dreary meal.

When the King talked, everybody else was forced to listen to him attentively.

Once or twice Gloria caught Prince Darius's eye and saw a distinct twinkle in it.

She felt that he was closely watching her reactions to everything that was said by the diners.

Because she knew she must behave with propriety, she concentrated on being extremely polite and attentive to the King.

And also to the Crown Prince who was sitting on her other side.

She was aware, however, that Prince Darius was making no effort to talk to the Crown Princess, who was on his left.

Nor did he bother with an extremely plain woman who was on his right. She wondered then why there were no other young people at the Court of the Kingdom of Arginos.

She then told herself that the King was so old that he must have retained the same people round him year after year.

He preferred it, rather than letting in strangers who might have opinions of their own.

The more she looked at The Palace, the more she realised how dull and unimaginative it was.

The building itself was magnificent so it was the furnishings that were so dreadfully dull and, of course, the people in it.

She was aware that the women of the Court were all dressed in gloomy tedious colours.

There was no doubt at all that her own gown, which was in the latest fashion, seemed sensational beside them.

She wondered what her mother would have thought if she had been here and what she would have advised her to do.

She recognised that, if she had not had that strange conversation with Prince Darius, she would have now been in deep despair.

It would be just impossible, she thought, to sit through many meals like the one that she was experiencing now.

Once again, the food was quite edible if unimaginative and poorly presented.

She noticed that the servants who waited on them, all seemed to be grey-haired except for a few young footmen.

When dinner was finally over, they moved into one of the larger Reception rooms. One of the women whom Gloria thought must be a Lady-in-Waiting walked over to the piano.

She played well, but she chose a rather gloomy and uninspiring Sonata.

It might well have been appropriate at a funeral.

She was followed by another lady who sang, but did not have a particularly good voice.

She chose a dreary operatic aria.

And it was with a sense of relief that the King then decided to retire for the night.

He bade his relatives 'goodnight', one by one, until he came to Gloria.

She sank down in a low curtsey and he then said,

"Goodnight, Lady Gloria. I very much hope that you have enjoyed your first evening at The Palace."

"Yes, indeed, Sire," Gloria replied, "it has been most interesting and informative."

It was just what the King wanted to hear.

He patted her on the shoulder before he walked away, the men bowing and the ladies curtseying until he had left the room.

Then the Crown Princess turned and suggested,

"I am very sure, Lady Gloria, that you will want to go to bed as tomorrow you have a very full programme."

Gloria looked at her questioningly.

"The first Deputation will be here, I think, at about ten o'clock," the Princess went on, "and after that you drive to Parliament, where you are to be received by the Prime Minister and his Cabinet."

As she finished speaking, the Crown Princess looked at Prince Darius.

He was standing nearby and she addressed him sharply,

"And don't be late, Darius, as you were the last time. It was very disconcerting besides being rude."

"Surely that happened four years ago or was it five?" Prince Darius remarked.

He spoke in a slow drawling voice.

Gloria thought that it proclaimed only too clearly how much he disliked his sister-in-law.

"Whenever it was," the Crown Princess said severely, "do *not* let it occur again. And do not forget, you will have to make a speech when you receive the gifts that the Cabinet and the Members of Parliament have all contributed to buy you."

"I only hope that it will be something I want," Prince Darius commented.

"Who would not want anything given to him or her so generously?" the Crown Princess asked sourly.

The Crown Prince came up at that moment and she said to him,

"I have just been telling Darius that he has to make a speech tomorrow and I hope you will convince him, Miklos, as I have failed to do, that he has to behave himself."

This was undoubtedly extremely rude of her.

Gloria was therefore not surprised when Prince Darius drawled,

"I think perhaps when it comes to politeness and good manners, my brother should start his lessons with his wife!"

Without saying anything more, he turned on his heel and walked out of the room.

The Princess gave an exasperated exclamation and Gloria said quickly,

"As I am very tired, I hope you will excuse me if I now retire to bed."

She curtseyed to the Crown Prince and then to the Crown Princess, before she walked towards the door.

There were a number of other people she had to say 'goodnight' to, although she had no idea who they were.

As she went upstairs, she thought that, if she did not have her way in anything else, she would not continue to live at The Palace.

She could not bear all this bickering and petty point scoring.

She was sure that the Crown Princess, who so obviously disliked Prince Darius, would, once they were married, be just as offensive to her.

It would be completely intolerable to have to see her day after day and have every meal at the same table, Gloria decided.

By the time she reached her bedroom, she was thinking that the Prince might fail to have enough money to buy or build a house in which case she was certain that her father would give them some as a Wedding present.

The Duke of Norwinton was in fact a very rich man.

Gloria had not spoken about it to the Prince, however, thinking that what he owned was insignificant compared to the Royal coffers.

But it would be surely enough for her to have her own way.

As she walked into her bedroom, she thought that it would be madness for them to even think of remaining in The Palace.

She knew it would be impossible to stay for month after month and year after year in a room that was so unattractively furnished.

It contained no colour and it was only then that she realised there were no flowers.

Her mother always had copious flowers in her bedroom both in summer and winter.

Now, Gloria thought, it was so typical of the gloom of The Palace that, while there were masses of beautiful flowers in the gardens, there were none inside.

'I want a house of my own and I don't care where it is or if it is very small,' she decided as she undressed. 'It will be filled with flowers and they at least will bring beauty and charm into any surroundings that I will have to endure.'

The maid who was attending to her said 'goodnight' and, after curtsying, left the room.

Gloria walked over to the windows to pull back the heavy and ugly curtains.

Outside, the stars filled the sky and the moon was steadily climbing up behind the trees and it made everything look very different from how it was in the daytime.

In fact the night held a mystic beauty, which she had not seen before in Arginos.

For a moment she forgot all about the dingy houses, the poorly-dressed people and the gloom of The Palace.

She looked up at the Heavens and felt almost as if the moonlight had a special message for her.

'Perhaps it will be – better than I – anticipated,' she whispered beneath her breath. 'Oh, *please God – let it be – better!*'

CHAPTER FIVE

The next morning Gloria received two Deputations of women one after the other.

The first came to petition her to do something about the Hospital.

"But surely you have one?" Gloria asked.

"We have, my Lady," the woman replied, "but it is very old-fashioned. We have none of the new instruments and medicines we read about, which they have in Greece and in other neighbouring countries."

"Is the King aware of this?" Gloria enquired.

"Oh, yes, my Lady, but he does not like anything that is new. He says that what was good enough for his father is good enough for him."

The next Deputation asked her to improve the schools for the younger children.

Apparently there were very few schools and the teachers were old and very scarce.

The children therefore had little chance of getting on well when they moved up into the more senior schools.

Again Gloria found that it was the King who thought that children could do quite well without being educated until they were ten years old.

She was feeling depressed as well as angry by the time the Deputations left.

She next put on her hat to be ready to drive to the Houses of Parliament.

She expected to find Prince Darius waiting for her.

Her heart sank when she saw that it was the Crown Prince.

"Where is your brother?" she enquired.

"There is no sign of him," the Crown Prince said crossly, "and the King has instructed me to go with you instead."

Gloria thought that Prince Darius was behaving very badly, but she knew that it would be a mistake for her to say so.

Instead she drove off with the Crown Prince and they were accompanied by an elderly woman whom she was told was her Lady-in-Waiting.

Today there were no crowds lining the route and the people walking about the streets did not appear to be very interested in her.

It occurred to Gloria that the large turn-out yesterday had obviously been contrived and orchestrated by The Palace

She guessed that the Union Jacks had been distributed amongst the children by Officials.

She thought that there was little point in discussing the matter with the Crown Prince.

They drove in silence until they reached the Houses of Parliament, which were indeed quite impressive.

They were received at the main entrance by the Prime Minister and his Cabinet.

They were then taken into a large hall where the Members of Parliament were all seated.

Once again Gloria was obliged to listen to the Prime Minister making a long and dreary speech.

He said the very same things that he had said yesterday, only more long-winded.

He was followed by the Secretary of State for Foreign Affairs of Arginos, who claimed that the whole idea of the Wedding to Queen Victoria's relative was his and his alone.

After he had finished, there were speeches by two other elderly men.

By this time Gloria had ceased to listen.

Instead she was thinking that it was most unfair of Prince Darius to have left her in the lurch at such a crucial moment.

She was not required to make a speech because she was a woman and the Crown Prince spoke on behalf of his brother.

He thanked the Houses of Parliament, explaining that Prince Darius was still somewhat indisposed after his long journey abroad.

He had, however, sent his most sincere apologies.

He also regretted he could not be present to thank them for all their congratulations and delightful presents.

These were a huge, rather ugly, silver punch bowl engraved with the Royal Coat of Arms and an oil painting of the Houses of Parliament.

As they drove back to The Palace, Gloria turned to the Crown Prince,

"I feel it would have been appropriate if I had said a few words about my forthcoming marriage as Prince Darius, who did not honour us with his presence at the Ceremony."

The Crown Prince looked at her in astonishment.

"You wish to speak?" he questioned.

"Why not?" she replied. "I could certainly make a better speech than those old gentlemen who were, I thought, extremely boring."

The Lady-in-Waiting, who had hardly said a word since they had left The Palace, gave a cry of consternation.

"You must not say things like that, my Lady," she expostulated. "I know that the Prime Minister would be very shocked."

"I can assure you that my father, the King, would not hear of any female of the Royal Family speaking in public!" the Crown Prince added. "It has never happened in the past and therefore cannot happen now!"

He spoke reprovingly as if Gloria was a small schoolgirl.

It made her wish that she had been brave enough to rise to her feet and speak before they could stop her.

They were eventually sitting down to luncheon when Prince Darius suddenly appeared in the dining room.

"Good morning, Papa," he said to his father. "Good morning, Lady Gloria."

He sat down in the empty seat next to her and she said to him in a low voice,

"I am very angry with you!"

"I thought you would be," he said, "but if I had come, I might well have made a scene and then you would have been ashamed of me."

Gloria could not help replying,

"It would at least have cheered things up."

"I knew you would find it deadly dull," he said. "They have not said anything new in the twenty-six years that I have known them!"

It was then that the King said in a voice of thunder,

"I hear, Darius, you did not go to Parliament this morning. Why not?"

"I was tired, Papa, after my long journey," the Prince said, "so I stayed in bed."

"It is disgraceful that your brother should have to take your place!" the King said angrily. "Utterly disgraceful! After all you are marrying the girl – not him!"

"I should hope not," Darius replied, "considering he has a wife already."

"That is not the way to answer me," the King thundered. "Have you apologised to your future wife?"

"She understands what I feel about the whole proceedings," Prince Darius said. "But if you wish to discuss it any further, Papa, I suggest we do so when we do not have such a large audience as we have now."

He spoke with an air of impertinence, which made the King splutter.

Then, as if he was aware that there were servants in the room, he did not say any more.

There was, however, Gloria thought, a gloom over luncheon, which made her glad when the meal ended.

As they all rose to their feet, one of the relatives who seemed nicer than the others came up to the Prince as if to placate him and said,

"I am longing to know, Darius, if you painted any more pictures on your last journey? I still treasure the one you gave me last Christmas."

"I have done one or two," the Prince replied vaguely.

"Then I look forward to seeing them," she answered.

She then had to step aside for Gloria to follow the King, who was leaving the room.

As the Prince walked beside her, she said,

"I did not know that you were an artist."

"I paint a little," he replied, "and, when I am travelling, I find it a good excuse to get into places which would otherwise be barred to an ordinary tourist."

"I never thought of that," Gloria exclaimed, "but I would love to see your pictures."

"Do you mean that," the Prince asked, "or are you just being polite?"

"I am being both," Gloria responded, which made him laugh.

When they reached the hall, the King walked towards the drawing room and the Prince said in a low voice,

"Unless you want to listen to my father scolding me yet again, I suggest that you come with me now and I will show you some of my paintings."

As he spoke, he started to move towards the staircase.

Gloria followed him, aware that for the moment the King had his back to them.

Feeling as if she was playing truant at school, she hurried to keep pace with the Prince.

When they reached the landing, they went up another staircase.

There were still more stairs to climb before they came to what Gloria knew must be the attics.

The walls slanted, but the Prince still proceeded until he opened a door at the far end.

Following him in, Gloria found herself in a large attic room with sloping ceilings on both sides.

But at the end there was a big wide window creating a North light.

There were paintings on canvas stacked against the walls and two or three pictures were on easels.

She looked around her exclaiming,

"So this is your studio!"

"It is also my excuse for escaping from the boredom downstairs," he added.

"Show me what you have painted," Gloria asked.

"This is the latest," he said. "I did it two months ago when I was in Turkey."

Looking at it Gloria realised that it was an unusual but original view of the Bosporus.

A cargo ship was passing down it and there were some small children swimming in the foreground.

She looked at it without speaking.

Then, realising that the Prince was watching her, she remarked,

"You really are an artist. It is not just pretence!"

"I try very hard," he said, "but you will understand that I have not only travelled to see the countries I depict, but also to enjoy the pictures that artists far better than I am have made of them."

"I think you are being unduly modest," Gloria said, "and, of course, you should have an Exhibition of your paintings."

The Prince held up his hands.

"Can you imagine what my father would say to that! I would be degrading the family and, of course, doing something that has never been done or even thought of before."

"I am sure these pictures," Gloria said, going from one to another, "would be appreciated not only by your own people but also by art lovers in other parts of the world."

"You are either flattering me or asking me in a rather roundabout way to paint a picture of you yourself," the Prince suggested.

"I am sure that is too much to expect," Gloria answered. "I am looking to see where the sketches are of alluring women, whom have doubtless sat for you in other countries."

She was teasing him and the Prince countered,

"I can set your mind at rest by saying that I really am a landscape artist."

"So I shall find nothing incriminating amongst all these canvasses?"

"I would doubt it and, if you are going to be a bossy jealous wife, I shall disappear the night before the Wedding!"

"You cannot frighten me," Gloria answered. "You know that is impossible and Queen Victoria would doubtless order you to be imprisoned in the Tower of London for the rest of your life!"

"I am almost inclined to risk it," the Prince said, "rather than go through the long dreary Ceremony we shall have to endure in the Cathedral. You have no idea how boring it will be."

"Every woman looks forward to her Wedding," she replied, "and I have a very beautiful Wedding gown. In fact I shall insist on taking it with me when we are on our honeymoon."

As she spoke, she had a sudden thought and asked him,

"We do go on honeymoon, I suppose?"

"To tell the truth, I have arranged nothing," the Prince answered, "because, as you know, I returned home only a week ago and was stunned by the news that I was to be married."

"We cannot stay in The Palace," Gloria cried in horror, "with everybody watching us and talking about us,"

"No, of course we cannot do that," the Prince agreed at once.

As he finished speaking, there came the sudden sound of footsteps.

They were running towards them along the passage that they had come to the studio by.

They were made by someone in a very great hurry and both Gloria and the Prince turned towards the door.

It was flung open and a young man came tearing in.

He had run so fast that he was very breathless.

For a moment he just stood there, panting for breath, before he said,

"They're at the gates, Your Royal Highness! They are trying to force their way into The Palace. You must get out quick!"

"I have been expecting this," the Prince said ruefully. "Has the King been told?"

"Yes, Your Royal Highness. They are all in a panic, but I knows you'd come up here and thinks you ought to be told what is happening."

"Thank you, Nuhar," the Prince said. "Now, get out yourself quickly and I will try and do the same."

The young man, who was little more than a boy, did not wait.

He turned and began to run back the way he had come.

The Prince took Gloria by the hand.

"Come on," he urged her. "We must not waste any time."

She had understood what the boy had said, but to make certain she asked,

"Has the Revolution started?"

"It has started," the Prince confirmed, "and it is going to be very unpleasant."

He did not say any more, but ran so rapidly down the stairs that speech was impossible.

The Prince took Gloria by some side-stairs to the second floor and into a bedroom that she knew was his.

He went to a chest of drawers, pulled open a drawer and took out some of his clothes.

Gloria stood feeling bewildered beside him and not knowing what to do.

Then he said,

"Take off your gown, turn it inside-out. You will find a handkerchief to cover your hair with in here. Hurry!"

Without saying any more, he went, carrying the clothes over his arms, through another door which opened off the bedroom.

Gloria had a glimpse of a washing stand and thought it must be for his *toilette*.

For a moment she could not understand what he had meant by saying that she should turn her gown inside out.

Then she realised that she was wearing one of the more elaborate gowns her mother had bought for her in London.

It was decorated with rows of lace and had a blue satin sash round the waist, which ended at the back in a bustle formed by a huge bow.

If they were to escape, she realised, she would be so conspicuous that she would not get very far.

She took off her gown as the Prince had instructed her to do.

She turned it inside-out, having first removed the sash and bustle.

It had a plain lining of a not particularly expensive material.

Remembering the women in their National dress, she left the bodice of the gown undone and pulled it away from her neck.

She next rolled up her sleeves so that her arms were bare to the elbow.

Having nothing round her waist, she looked through the chest of drawers where there were several plain leather belts and she chose one which seemed the widest.

It was large, but it gave her a tidier appearance.

She then pulled out a large silk handkerchief and she had the idea that, when the Prince was being an artist, he would tie one round his neck.

She chose a blue one, which she tied at the back of her neck and which covered her hair.

She had only just finished arranging it in front of the mirror, when the door opened.

The Prince came back into the room and was looking very different.

He had discarded the white Military coat and trousers he had worn at the luncheon party.

Instead, he was wearing a very old pair and his shirt, that wanted washing, was open at the neck and his sleeves were rolled up.

He wore a belt round his waist and he carried in his hand a coat that was of well-worn almost threadbare velvet.

Gloria took a quick glance at him and then gave an exclamation.

The Prince had not only changed his clothes, he had shaved off his moustache.

It made him look very different, in fact, far more handsome than he had before.

"You have removed your moustache," she exclaimed.

"Not only because I hope not to be recognised," he explained, "but also because I wore it as my father insisted that my brother and I should look Military."

He was opening another drawer as he spoke.

She saw him take out a purse. He put it into his pocket and then produced a wallet.

He saw her watching him and said,

"At least we will have some money to get on with. Now, come on. We have to escape by a side exit."

"There is only one thing," Gloria said, "I am afraid my slippers might give me away and I do not want to walk barefoot."

She put out a foot as she spoke.

The Prince saw that she was wearing blue satin slippers, which had matched her sash.

He hesitated.

Then he drew from another drawer a pair of grey woollen socks.

He pulled them on over her shoes and she looked like a peasant girl who had just come in from the fields.

The Prince put out his hand and, taking hers, he drew her to the door.

He listened, but there was no sign of anybody outside, so he opened it.

*

Afterwards they flew, rather than walked, along many dusty corridors and down small dark side-staircases.

Finally they reached the side of The Palace where there was no sign or sound of any Revolutionaries.

On their way they passed one door, which opened towards the kitchens.

Gloria saw that there was no one there and she guessed that the servants had run away in haste.

The Prince then opened a door that was bolted on the inside and they stepped out into the garden.

As it was right on the side of The Palace and near to the tradesmen's entrance, there were no flowers only shrubs.

The Prince drew Gloria through them.

He was walking quickly and steadily without hesitating as if he knew exactly what he was doing.

They came to what she realised was a side gate to The Palace.

There should have been sentries in the boxes on each side of it, but, when the Prince looked for them, they were not there.

"We are in luck," he said.

They were the first words he had spoken since they had left his bedroom.

Walking steadily, as if there was no hurry, he moved Gloria through the gates and out into the street.

Only then did he quicken his pace and hurry away from The Palace just as swiftly as he could.

They had walked for about five minutes when there was the sound of loud voices.

The Prince stopped.

There were just a few houses ahead with gardens encircled by high hedges.

The Prince opened the gate nearest to them and drew Gloria inside.

There was still nobody to be seen, but he moved her behind the hedge that bordered the road.

It was then that she began to feel really frightened.

The noise of voices was coming nearer and a few seconds later she could see, by peeping through the hedge, a crowd of men and boys who were running down the road.

They were all carrying sticks and the one leading them was shouting,

"The Palace, The Palace – this way to The Palace!"

Every time he spoke, those behind him shouted,

"To The Palace!"

"Down with the King!"

"Kill him! *Kill him*!"

Although the crowd were mostly very young and unfledged, they were intimidating.

Gloria moved a little closer to the Prince as if asking him to protect her.

He did not speak, he only put his arm round her shoulders to reassure her that he was there.

When she glanced at him as he watched the crowd pass, his face was grim.

It did not take long and, when they were gone, he urged,

"Come on, we must get out of here in case anyone recognises us."

He started to run and so it was impossible for Gloria to ask him questions.

She only picked up her skirts so that she could run beside him.

He seemed to know the way and they turned down one road, then another.

Finally there were no more houses and they were now out in the countryside.

At any other time Gloria would have thought it very lovely.

The uncultivated fields sloped away towards the river and in the distance she could see that there was a high range of mountains and some appeared still to have snow on their peaks.

She was, however, breathless from the speed that they had been running at.

She could only stand, breathing deeply.

At the same time she was wondering what would happen to them and where they would go.

The Prince was looking ahead as if he was deciding what would be the safest direction for them to travel in.

Finally he said,

"We had better move on. It would be a mistake to linger here and so far nobody seems to have noticed us."

"Where are we – going?" Gloria asked nervously.

She thought that it was a foolish question even as she asked it.

Whatever the Prince replied, it would mean nothing to her.

"Away from what is happening at The Palace," the Prince replied. "We are lucky not to have been caught in a trap."

"Do you think – they will really kill your – father?" Gloria asked.

"I don't think our own people would do so," the Prince answered, "but there were a number of Russians amongst those who have just passed by."

"And they will – incite the others to kill anyone – who is Royal," Gloria murmured.

She was thinking as she spoke that it might be herself.

If she had not gone up the stairs to the Prince's studio with him, she would have been in the drawing room with the King and his other relations.

They were walking very quickly, but she managed to say,

"Surely the soldiers will – fire on the – intruders to keep them – away?"

"It is possible," the Prince answered, "but the Russians plan their Revolutions extremely cleverly. They make sure that everybody, whatever their position in life, has a grievance that they believe will be put right if the Rulers of the country concerned are eliminated."

There was nothing that Gloria could answer to this and they walked on in silence.

The ground was dry and it was not as hot as it had seemed yesterday.

In fact there was a breeze coming from the river, which was a good antidote to the heat of the sun.

They walked and walked.

Finally, when Gloria looked back, The Palace was no longer in sight, nor was the City of Koloni.

"Are you feeling tired?" the Prince asked her unexpectedly.

"A little," Gloria answered, "and my socks are beginning to wear away so that they will no longer conceal my shoes."

The Prince looked up at the sky.

The sun was very low now and the shadows of the trees were becoming longer.

"We will find somewhere to stay," he said. "I suppose the best thing would be for you to pretend to be my wife."

Gloria was about to ask him why, but then she knew the answer for herself.

People would be suspicious of a young man with a pretty young woman.

In point of fact they would refuse to give them shelter if they felt that there was anything improper in their relationship.

She was just about to say that perhaps it would be easier if she was his sister and then she realised that his hair was dark while she was very fair.

"I am prepared to agree to anything," she said aloud, "so long as we find somewhere to sleep. I don't particularly fancy a ditch!"

"Nor do I," the Prince agreed, "and, as you know, I have brought some money with me."

"Have you really been wise enough to prepare for this Revolution?" Gloria asked.

"Every time that I have come home I have realised that the situation has become more explosive," the Prince replied. "As I have already said, my father would not listen to anything I have told him. So I had to take certain precautions in order not to be caught completely unawares."

He smiled before he added,

"I certainly did not expect to have the encumbrance of a 'wife' with me!"

"What you are really saying," Gloria remarked, "is that you would have left me behind and just vanished as you have before, only on this occasion to safety."

"Then I could hardly have spirited away the whole of my relations," the Prince said. "My father and brother have brought it all on themselves. I did try to warn them."

Gloria suddenly thought that the way he was speaking sounded pathetic and plaintive.

She could well understand the frustration he must have felt when he was laughed at and his advice ignored.

"I can only say that I am very glad that I asked to see your paintings – when I did," she said.

"I am afraid that you are not going to find being a fugitive particularly comfortable," the Prince answered. "We must take very great care not to be recognised."

"You mean – the Russians or the Revolutionaries will be – looking for – us?"

The Prince shrugged his shoulders.

"They may be and I can assure you that I have no wish to be taken back to Koloni for – questioning."

Gloria shivered.

She knew enough about the Russian Third Section to understand that an interrogation in Russia was a terrifying experience.

It usually resulted in torture if not death.

Because she was frightened, she slipped her hand into the Prince's.

"Please," she begged, "tell me – what to do. I do *not* want to make any – mistakes."

"Just leave everything to me," he said, "and then talk as little as possible. You speak our language well, but your voice is educated and that is suspicious in itself."

She realised that he had thought this all out and she merely nodded as he went on,

"I suppose, really, I should try and get you out of the country, but I want to know what is happening at The Palace."

"And, of course, if possible, you will want to save your people from being under Russian domination from now on."

"You really think that I could do something like that?" the Prince asked.

"I do not know how," Gloria replied, "but I feel very strongly that the only person who could do anything in this dreadful situation would be *you*."

"You surprise me," the Prince exclaimed.

He did not say anything more.

She had the feeling, however, that she had made him think and they walked on in silence.

They came to a small out-of-the-way village that was picturesque and charming.

Gloria saw that the people were entirely agricultural as there were only peasant houses.

The men they saw moving along the road were very obviously returning from their work in the fields.

Then, just ahead of them, there was a larger building.

Gloria knew from the long wooden table set outside that it was an inn.

"This will have to do," the Prince said beneath his breath. "Keep your head down and say nothing."

It was a precise order and Gloria obeyed him.

They walked into the inn.

Speaking in a different voice from the one he usually used, the Prince went up to what was obviously a bar and said to the man standing behind it,

"There be a lot of trouble goin' on in the City. Do you know what it be all about?"

"Trouble?" the man behind the bar asked. "What d'you mean – trouble?"

"There's shoutin' and shootin'," the Prince said firmly. "and people rushin' about in all directions. I've brought me wife away. We be here on holiday and we don't want no trouble."

"That be right sensible of you," the other man replied. "I wonder what's a-goin' on?"

"Maybe it's somethin' – maybe nothin'!" the Prince said enigmatically. "But we'd rather stay here, if you'll have us."

"I've got one room," the man who was obviously the Proprietor replied, "but it'll cost you three *drachma*."

Gloria knew that this was very cheap, but the Prince hesitated,

"I thinks I can manage that all right," he said after a pause, "and we both be hungry if there's some dinner?"

"Ye can have what me wife's cookin' and be welcome," the Proprietor said, "but it ain't anythin' fancy."

"I never did care for fancy food meself," the Prince replied, "but thank you for lettin' us stay. I don't like Cities and certainly not when there's trouble there."

"I don't know about any trouble," the Proprietor said. "There's bin a bit of talk round 'ere, but then – is there ever anythin' else?"

"I suppose not," the Prince agreed. "People talk and talk, but things go on just the same as they ever was."

"Where've you come from?" the Proprietor enquired.

The Prince named a place that Gloria thought was somewhere on the coast.

"Oh, there!" the Proprietor exclaimed. "Then I expect you work in the shipyard?"

"I does when there's any work to be had," the Prince replied. "Trouble is, they don't build enough ships these days."

"That be true," the Proprietor agreed. "It's said we're gettin' behind other countries in many ways."

"That's just what I've been tellin' the wife," the Prince replied.

"Well, come on and I'll show you the room," the Proprietor suggested.

They went up the bare rickety stairs to the first floor.

At the top of the stairs were what appeared to be two rooms and Gloria thought that the Proprietor and his wife probably slept in one of them.

In the other and the door was open, she could see that, like the Prince's studio, there were sloping ceilings.

Standing against one wall was a double bed with a wooden headboard.

There were no rugs on the floor and there was a chest of drawers with a cracked mirror on the wall behind it and two hardback chairs.

In front of the window stood a table with a china basin and a ewer.

That completed the contents of the room.

"This'll do us fine," the Prince exclaimed.

The Proprietor held out his hand.

"I'll have the money in advance," he said. "I find folks is often unable to pay or they leaves without doin' so after enjoyin' me hospitality."

The Prince laughed.

"I'd not do that to you."

He then drew some small coins from his pocket and counted them out slowly into the proprietor's hand.

When the amount was complete, he closed his fingers over it.

"Thank you," he said, "and I'll tell the wife you'll be wantin' a bite to eat. "It'll be ready soon."

"We won't be late," the Prince answered.

The Proprietor left the room, going slowly down the stairs, step by step.

When he was out of hearing, Gloria looked at the Prince and he looked at her.

"We have – escaped," she whispered.

"By the skin of our teeth!" the Prince replied. "And touch wood. It is unlucky to boast."

There was a note in his voice that made Gloria shiver.

She knew without him saying so that he was still afraid that they might be discovered.

She had a feeling that if they were, it would be her fault, and the Prince would be far safer on his own.

"Thank you – for – bringing me," she said to him in a very small voice.

CHAPTER SIX

Gloria dreamt that she was being kissed.

It was exactly what she thought a kiss would be like.

She could feel little quivers of excitement running through her body and ending in her lips.

As she awakened, she remembered what had happened last night.

They had enjoyed quite a good meal, cooked by the Proprietor's wife, and then they went upstairs.

For the first time Gloria felt shy and more than a little embarrassed.

"What are – we to do – about the – bed?" she asked. "Shall we take it in turns, two or three hours at a time, or perhaps we could – make up a – bed on the floor?"

"I have a better idea than that," the Prince replied.

"I will go for a walk while you get into bed. When I come back, I will sleep on top of the opposite side. You will not even realise that I am there."

He smiled before he added,

"I do not snore and I hope that you can say the same!"

Before Gloria could reply that she was sure that she did not snore, he was gone.

For a short moment she felt that it was all very irregular and something that her father and mother would heartily disapprove of.

Then she told herself that the Prince did not like her and she did not like him.

Therefore there was no need in any way to think of him as if he was a young man who was interested in her.

She also felt so tired that it was impossible to argue or to refuse what he had – ordained.

That was the right word, she ruminated, as she started to undress.

He had ordered her to do what he wanted and so it would be best to obey him.

She took off her gown and put it over one of the chairs.

Having washed in cold water and, wearing only her chemise, she climbed into the bed.

She lay down on the very edge of the side that she had chosen.

And almost as soon as her head touched the pillow she fell fast asleep.

The day's adventures and fears all slipped through her mind as a jumble.

Now, as her dream about being kissed ended rather suddenly, she opened her eyes.

The Prince was standing beside the bed, already dressed.

She looked up at him and he asserted,

"Get up and hurry! We have a great deal to do."

"What? What do we – have to – do?" Gloria stammered sleepily.

"I will tell you later," he answered, "but now I am going to order our breakfast."

He went from the room and Gloria got out of bed.

She found that, although the Prince had washed in the basin, he had thrown the dirty water away.

The ewer was half-full and she thought how pleasant it would be to have a nice hot bath.

Then she laughed at the idea of what a commotion it would cause in the inn.

She dressed, thinking that the inside of her beautiful gown looked somewhat dilapidated after yesterday.

But there was nothing that she could do about it now.

She covered her hair with the handkerchief and then hurried downstairs.

The Prince was already sitting at the table where they had eaten dinner the night before.

The Proprietor's wife was in the process of bringing him a breakfast of eggs and bacon, which smelled delicious.

When she had gone to bring the same for Gloria, she said,

"We are having a very English breakfast."

"I thought we had better sustain ourselves," the Prince answered, "in case we have to wait or go without our luncheon."

"Where are we going now?" Gloria asked him.

"I will tell you when we have finished eating," he said.

She thought that he was being careful in case she said something that might be overheard by the Proprietor's wife.

She ate her eggs and bacon, which she thought were superb and drank the coffee, which was of an inferior quality.

However, she thought it would be sustaining.

After breakfast she went upstairs to make certain that they had not left anything behind.

When she came down again, she found that the Prince was standing in the hall waiting rather impatiently for her.

To her surprise he had put on the coat that he had carried yesterday and it certainly made him look like very much the artist.

He had tied a red handkerchief round his neck.

He did not speak when she appeared, but took her arm and led her rapidly out of the inn.

He walked quickly and, when they were out of earshot, she said,

"Please tell me where we are going and why we are in such a hurry."

"We are going to be married," he answered.

Gloria stopped dead.

"Are you – joking?"

"No, I have already arranged it with a Priest in a small Church, which is a little further on."

"But – why? I do not – understand," Gloria quavered.

The Prince looked at her and smiled.

"I am a man, Gloria," he replied, "and, if you think I could sleep as we did last night without telling you how lovely you are, you are very much mistaken!"

She thought that she must still be dreaming.

Could he really be saying this to her?

And yet there was an expression in his eyes that she had not seen before.

"I-I don't – understand," she mumbled in a small voice.

"I will explain it to you once we are married," he said. "You came to this country to marry me and the sooner I am under the protection of the Union Jack the better!"

He spoke lightly, but she still could not understand why they were being married in such haste.

And what had he meant by saying that he could not sleep beside her?

He started to walk on, and there was nothing she could do but keep pace with him.

A few minutes later she saw the Church straight ahead of them.

It was very small and she thought very old.

Like the Cathedral in which she was to have been married in Koloni, it belonged to the Greek Church.

She had, however, been told that there were certain variations in the Services.

Only as they reached the Church porch did Gloria say,

"You – you kissed – me this morning – it was – not a dream."

"I thought it was the best way of waking you up," the Prince replied.

He smiled as he spoke.

She felt the same strange quiver running through her that she had felt when his lips had touched hers while she was still asleep.

There was nothing more she could say.

He opened the Church door and they walked in.

It was even smaller inside than she had imagined.

A Priest stood in front of the Altar and she could feel an atmosphere of sanctity that she had not felt in many other Churches.

The Prince then offered her his arm.

When she put her hand on it, he drew her up the aisle towards the Priest.

The Service was a short one, but Gloria understood every word of what was said.

When finally they received the Blessing, the Priest gave it with a sincerity that made her feel that they were actually being blessed by God Himself.

It made her feel that she need not be quite so frightened of the future as she was at the moment.

They rose as the Priest knelt before the Altar.

The Prince then placed some money on the Communion Table in the Transept.

Without speaking, he took Gloria's hand and they walked down the aisle and out into the sunshine.

She felt his fingers tighten on hers.

She thought that no woman could have had a more unexpected and unusual Wedding.

They walked hand-in-hand for nearly half-an-hour before the Prince said,

"I have been told that there are some soldiers stationed a little way from here. They are on manoeuvres and I am going to try and find out if I can trust them."

Gloria stared at him in astonishment.

"Trust – them?" she exclaimed. "But suppose they too – are part of the Revolution? They might – kill you."

"I shall have to risk it," he said, "but I think it only fair to tell you what I am doing."

Gloria stopped.

"Listen to – me," she pleaded. "Please – please listen to – me."

"I am listening," the Prince answered.

"You must not take any risks," she urged. "You heard those men who – passed us saying that they – intended to – kill the King. If they – kill you – then there will be – nobody left in the country to – try and prevent the Russians from – taking over."

"I am aware of that," the Prince replied, "but, if I can persuade some of our own troops to follow me, then we can save Arginos."

He spoke with an iron determination that Gloria knew she would not be able to change.

She looked up at him pleadingly.

"Please – be very – very careful."

He put his arms round her.

"I will be, because I want to be with you," he said. "And I want to teach you, my lovely darling, about Love."

He kissed her then and she knew that what she had felt before was not a dream, but an ecstasy beyond words.

He kissed her until she felt that they were both flying in the sky.

There were no dangers, no problems, no Revolutions, only *Love*.

Abruptly the Prince set her free.

"There is so much I have to do," he said, "and you must not tempt me as you are doing at this moment."

Because it was such an unexpected thing for him to say, Gloria laughed.

"Can it be possible that we ever – hated each other?" she asked. "Now suddenly I know that your – kiss is the most – wonderful thing in the – whole world."

"I kissed you this morning," the Prince said, "because I could not help it and I want to spend the rest of the day and, of course, the night kissing you, but first *we* have to do our duty."

He accentuated the word *we* as he had done before.

Gloria bit back the words she wanted to say, begging him to kiss her again rather than go into danger.

But there was an expression on the Prince's face that told her she must not interfere.

They walked on quickly and in silence.

Then, when they had passed through some tall trees, they saw directly below them, on the ground sloping down to a stream, that there were a large number of men.

They were mostly in uniform, but there were some country men amongst them.

They were reclining on the grass.

Standing just above them, with his back to Gloria and the Prince, was a man who was speaking to them.

As they drew a little nearer, Gloria could hear what he was saying.

She also realised that once that he was not an Arginosian.

He was telling the men how they could achieve their freedom, how they could demolish the authority of the Politicians, their Statesmen and the King.

As she listened, Gloria knew with a feeling of horror that this was one of the Russians causing the Revolution.

He was inciting the men listening to him, and she reckoned that there were well over a hundred, to go with him to Koloni.

There they would kill and smash up almost everything that was there.

"The choice is yours," the Russian finished, "either you become free of your bonds, killing those who give you orders or you remain as you are, slaves to your

King, a King who does not worry about you and does not care whether you live or you die."

He finished speaking.

Before Gloria could take a breath, the Prince ran down the hill to stand beside him.

"Before you make any decisions," he said to the men listening, "I think you should hear the other side of the coin. I am one of you, I am an Arginosian and I ask you to hear me and listen intently as you have listened to this Revolutionary who has just put his case to you."

At his sudden appearance, the men who had been lounging on the ground sat up straight.

Gloria was surprised when one of them shouted out,

"All right then, let's hear you. What have you got to say?"

The Prince moved a little nearer to them.

He was aware, as he did so, that the Russian was wondering what he should do about him.

Finally, with bad grace, he sat down on the ground, glaring at the intruder yet feeling that he was too insignificant to be of any real danger.

Gloria walked a little nearer, but still kept in the background.

She sat down on the grass just as the Prince began to speak.

To her surprise he spoke extremely well.

He threw his voice far better than the Russian had been able to do, so that everybody at the back of the crowd could hear him clearly and every word he spoke.

He also had a very musical almost mesmeric voice that she had not noticed before.

She knew immediately that with his first sentence he had captured the men's attention.

He spoke very simply.

He told them how he loved his country as he was sure that they did as well.

But changes needed to be made which would be to the benefit of every man, woman and child in the country of Arginos.

He agreed absolutely that the present *régime* was out of date.

The country was behind its neighbours in innovations, progress and new ideas.

But there was nothing so wrong that it could not be put right.

"What we require," he said, "is a large Army and Navy. The prosperity of this country rests on the workers in the fields who can sell their goods overseas at good prices."

"What have we got to sell?" someone shouted.

It was a man who was not in uniform.

"For one thing – food," the Prince replied. "I have just been in Turkey, where they are exporting fruit in large quantities to Greece, who is next door to us and many other countries in the Balkans.

"I believe that we have the best peaches and the finest figs here in Arginos and, if we plant vines, I am sure that we can produce excellent grapes which can be made into delicious wine."

He paused for a moment to catch his breath.

Then he went on,

"We have never explored our mountains for gold, which I am sure is there, together with many other minerals which, if we can find them, will make us all very rich."

"How can you be sure of that?" the Russian, whose place he had taken, snarled.

"I am sure it can be done," the Prince replied, "just as I am sure that you and your people will take these men into slavery."

He turned to the audience as he spoke and said,

"Do you realise you have been listening to Russian propaganda? Russians who treat their serfs like slaves. You cannot be so ignorant as not to be aware that the serfs own nothing, but they themselves are owned by their Masters.

"If they do not obey them, they can be killed without any protests to the Czar or anyone else. Is that what you want to happen in this beautiful country of ours?"

There was then a low murmur from the listeners.

Gloria saw that the Russian who had been speaking drew something from his pocket.

It was a revolver, but before he could raise it, she gave a scream and ran towards the Prince.

As she did so, one of the soldiers lifted his rifle and shot the Russian through his heart.

As he fell back dead, Gloria reached the Prince as he said,

"Like all Russians, that man is one of a kind who has penetrated into our country and is at the moment destroying our City and a great number of people in it."

As he spoke, three men, who from their appearance were also Russians, rose from the crowd and started to run away.

They had not gone far before the soldiers shot them all down.

Gloria was holding onto the Prince's left arm.

He did not look at her, but only said to the soldiers,

"So perish all those who try to deceive us! I want to go to the City. Will you follow me and help me clear out these rats who are trying to destroy all that we stand for?"

Several of the men rose to their feet and started to cheer.

An Officer appeared from the far end of the crowd.

Gloria thought that she had seen him arrive while the Prince was speaking.

He walked through the crowd of cheering men up to the Prince and when he reached him he exclaimed,

"Surely, you are Prince Darius?"

The Prince looked at him.

"Good Heavens, it is you, Makius!"

He held out his hand and the Officer shook it.

"You were extremely brave," he said. "I too had wanted to intervene but was not quite certain whether or not the men would listen. But they listened to you, so I suppose we had better go to Koloni now."

"I will take you," Darius said in a tone of authority.

He looked down at Gloria as if he suddenly realised that she was there.

"This is Captain Makius," he said to her. "He was at school with me and is, I know, a very able Officer in what is left of our Army."

The Captain frowned.

"Are you rebelling in Koloni from your family?"

The Prince nodded.

"That is why I left," he said. "This is my wife, who is English. We can therefore be sure of some support, if it comes in time, from the British."

"Thank God for that!" the Captain exclaimed. "Do you want the men to know who you are?"

"Better not," the Prince said, "not until we see what is happening in the City."

"Well, tell them what you want, because they are obviously going to follow you," the Captain said.

The Prince moved nearer to the men, who were standing a little way away.

"We are going to the City," he said. "I want to know if all of you are ready to deal with the Russians who are already there and will be breaking up The Palace and, I imagine, many other of our fine buildings.

"As I promised you, there will be changes, which will all be for the best. But first we have to get rid of our enemies and the quicker the better."

Then the Captain produced three horses, one for himself, one for the Prince and one for Gloria.

As the Prince lifted her onto the saddle, the Captain said,

"Two of these horses belonged to the Russians, so at least they have been of some help."

"I am grateful that my wife does not have to walk," the Prince replied.

They moved off, the soldiers putting on their caps and carrying their weapons.

Gloria noticed that behind them there were thirty or forty country men.

Those who had not a heavy stick picked one up as they passed through the woods.

Then they were on a road that Gloria thought would take them directly to the City.

It would very obviously be far quicker than the way that she and the Prince had come yesterday, because they were in hiding.

They certainly looked very strange.

The Prince had taken off his velvet coat and was riding in his shirtsleeves.

The Officer, however, looked very smart in his uniform.

As they passed through several small villages, men came out to stare at them.

When both the soldiers and the country men shouted out what they were going to do, they joined in.

The women waved them goodbye and Gloria saw that some of them were in tears.

It was obvious that those in this part of the country knew what was happening.

Although they had been too afraid to voice their fears, they had no wish to be under the Russian yoke.

They moved on, not going too fast, because the men were walking behind them.

"Have those in command of the Army any idea of what the Russians were planning?" the Prince said to Captain Makius.

"They have been warned," the Captain answered, "but they did not want to listen."

The Prince thought that might be said of his father and brother, the Prime Minister and everyone else in authority in the country.

He could only pray that he was not too late to prevent the Revolutionaries from taking over.

It took them two hours to reach the outskirts of the City.

When the outer walls were only a little way ahead, the Prince stopped.

He told the men to rest for a few minutes and then to load their rifles.

By this time the followers had swollen to over a hundred with more joining all the time.

"We have no idea what we are up against," the Prince told them, "but every one of you must be on your guard. The Russians can win only if there is no opposition. They will not yet be here in great numbers, but we can be certain that their troops are not far away, ready to march in to restore order. They will then be in possession of the whole of our country."

"They'll not do that!" the men shouted out.

The Prince replied quietly,

"It is up to you, every one of you."

He then gave the order to move and the soldiers marched in line while the other men followed them.

They looked formidable and aggressive, Gloria thought.

Nevertheless she was still very frightened, especially for the Prince, who rode on ahead unarmed.

He was obviously an easy target.

The gates of the City were open and there were no sentries as there should have been.

Inside the walls the people stared in astonishment.

When they became aware of what was happening, a number of men and boys joined the marchers.

By the time they reached the central Square, their numbers had swelled considerably.

It was then that Gloria saw with a sinking of her heart that the square was already half-full.

There was a man standing on the plinth of a large statue, haranguing them.

He was Russian.

What he was saying was clearly intended to incite his listeners into taking action against the authorities.

When he saw the Prince and Captain Makius, followed by the troops and country men, ride into the Square, he shouted,

"Here they come! The people who imprison and crush you into the ground! *Kill them*! Make them run for their lives and kill th – !"

Before he could finish speaking. Captain Makius drew his revolver and shot him.

He crumpled and fell from where he was standing onto the ground.

For a moment there was a shocked silence.

Then everybody began to shout and screech out at the same time.

With a quickness that could only have been taken by a man who was athletically strong, the Prince leapt from his horse.

He climbed up onto the base of the statue in the centre of the Square.

For a moment he just stood there, waiting for the noise to abate.

He raised his hand and at last the shouting and protesting died away.

"My friends," he shouted, "the man who has just been killed is a Russian who has been deceiving you. He and his fellow countrymen will not save you as he promised but lead you into a bondage more terrible than anything you have ever envisaged."

He then spoke again about the Russian serfs and he continued to tell how Arginos could move with the times and become rich and of considerable importance in the world.

As he had said before, he added,

"We want to increase our Army and Navy with men who are young, adventurous and ready to protect Arginos from anybody who attempts to conquer us, however subtly they may try to do it."

He told them too how they could become very prosperous with what hitherto had been undeveloped and ignored.

"It is up to each one of you," he said. "I know that every man here wants his children to inherit a far better country than we have had up until now. We have to move with the times. We have to have new inventions and mountains of new ideas."

It was then that somebody interrupted him.

A man spoke something quietly to him and the Prince bent down to hear him.

The people were beginning to talk amongst themselves again and he stood upright and raised his hand for silence.

"I have just learnt," he said, "that my father, the King, died of a heart attack yesterday when the Revolutionaries invaded The Palace. My brother, the Crown Prince, was killed. I am Prince Darius and I ask you to accept me in my rightful place as your King. If you will do that, I swear to you that everything I have just said will be put into operation. With your help we shall have new ships, new industries, better schools and what my wife has already asked me to provide for you, a larger and much more up to date modern Hospital."

Almost before he said the last words, the people were cheering.

Once again, Gloria, who was watching the crowd intently, suddenly saw a man draw out a revolver from his jacket pocket.

She screamed and pointed at him.

Before he could use it, an Arginosian who was standing next to him knocked him to the ground.

Several other men then beat him over the head with their sticks.

As the noise subsided, the Prince said,

"There are more Russians amongst you. If we are to get anywhere and if we are to put into operation my ideas for the future, I must remain alive. So I am asking you, my people, to save me from these foreigners who want your King dead."

There were cries of,

"We will!" *"We will!"*

As several shifty-looking men then started to move away through the crowd, they were knocked down or shot by the soldiers.

The Prince did not move.

He merely stood watching, while the huge crowd screamed as one man after another was eliminated.

When there appeared to be no foreigners left standing, the Prince said,

"Thank you. Now we start from this moment to make our country a decent place to live in. This City must become a place that each one of us can be proud of."

He looked down at the listening people before he continued,

"I want every able-bodied man who does not wish to or is too old to join my Army and Navy to start immediately building larger and better houses and more important shops. They will be paid, every one of them, for the work they do. Tomorrow morning I shall be waiting in The Palace to receive anyone who comes to me with new ideas that will improve the City and our beautiful country."

There were more cheers at this.

Then he went on,

"I think during that brief and unpleasant Revolution created by the Russians, not only The Palace but also a number of shops and perhaps houses will have been damaged. Let me assure their owners that they will receive full compensation from the State. If they will bring their estimates to me, I will deal with them all personally."

Now the people were cheering wildly and the Prince bent forward towards Gloria.

One of the soldiers lifted her from the saddle of the horse that she was sitting on and up onto the base of the statue to stand beside the Prince.

As she did so, he took off the silk handkerchief that covered her head and the sunshine turned her hair into a shining halo.

"I want to present to you," the Prince said, raising his voice above the tumult, "my wife. As you know, she has come from England, a relative of Queen Victoria's, so that we have the support of the British Empire now. I know that my wife already wishes to help you as she has helped me. She as well will be waiting tomorrow to receive a Deputation of any ladies who require anything special for the children of this City."

There were more cheers at this and Gloria waved her hand.

Then the Prince climbed down and lifted her back onto her horse.

They now rode through the crowd, followed by Captain Makius and some of the soldiers.

It was a triumphant ride with the people running beside them, shouting excitedly all the way to The Palace.

It was only as they arrived there that Gloria wondered apprehensively what they would find.

It took them some time to make their way to the front entrance.

They had to keep stopping on the steps to turn and wave to the cheering crowd.

There were still no sentries on the steps and this enabled a number of people to follow them right up almost to the door of The Palace itself.

The Prince turned round once again to wave.

As he did so, Captain Makius and a few soldiers prevented anybody else from following them as they walked inside.

The first thing Gloria saw was a tumult of wreckage and untidiness.

The curtains had been pulled down from the windows and there were blood stains on the floor.

Papers were scattered everywhere and a number of window panes had been smashed.

There were, however, no dead bodies, which she had been afraid to see.

As the Prince walked in, some of the older servants, who must have been in hiding, came hurrying into the hall.

Some were not in their Livery. They all bowed respectfully to the Prince.

"What has happened to the Ladies of the Court?" the Prince asked.

"They ran to the British Embassy, Your Royal Highness."

Before the Prince could ask another question, Captain Makius said,

"I have just been told, Sir, that the British Embassy was untouched."

The Prince smiled at Gloria and murmured,

"The power of the Union Jack!"

Then he enquired,

"Has any real damage been done here?"

"No, Your Royal Highness," one of the old servants replied. "They've robbed a great many items that were portable, but The Palace wasn't set on fire, as was suggested at first."

"And His Majesty's body?" the Prince enquired.

"Lyin' at rest in the Chapel, Sir, as be that of the Crown Prince."

The servant had hardly finished speaking when a number of others then appeared and the Prince said,

"A great deal has been done in the last few hours. My wife and I are both hungry, as are Captain Makius, and the soldiers who accompanied us to The Palace. Will you ask everyone who can cook to arrange a buffet in the dining room as quickly as they can provide us with food?"

Gloria wanted to laugh at the astonishment on the servants' faces.

The one who had been speaking then said,

"I thinks, Your Royal Highness, there be little food left. Them thieves took the lot."

The Prince pulled out his purse.

"Buy what is necessary," he ordered.

Captain Makius bent towards the Prince and said in a low voice,

"There is no need to be so generous, Sir. My men will find something elsewhere."

"They will eat here!" the Prince replied. "It will be an experience for them if nothing else. Put several sentries on the steps to prevent us from being interrupted. Your men can come up in turn as soon as the food is cooked and ready."

Captain Makius laughed.

"If anyone is causing a Revolution, Your Majesty, it is you!"

"You will have to get used to me," the Prince replied, "because you are now in command of the Army."

Captain Makius stared at him.

"Do you mean that, Sir?"

"I want a young Army, an adventurous one, and one I can trust," the Prince said. "As you qualify for all those things, Makius, I can only ask you to start things going immediately in your new position as Commander-in-Chief."

Captain Makius smiled.

"I am very grateful, Sir. You know I will serve Your Majesty to the best of my ability for the rest of my life!"

The way he spoke was very moving.

The Prince then looked at Gloria.

"I think," he said, "the least we can do before we start entertaining our guests is to make ourselves look a little more conventional. I hope we have something left. The only thing we can do is to go and see."

Gloria laughed and they ran up the stairs together holding hands.

She noticed that the stair carpet had been left because it was too large for anyone to carry away.

But the curtains, which she had always thought very ugly, had gone, as had some of the smaller pictures.

She was quite certain that there would be no *objets d'art* left in the Reception rooms.

The sconces that held the candles had been taken from the walls in the corridors.

She next went into her bedroom.

She was not surprised to find that the curtains had been ripped down from the windows and the bed.

There were several chairs missing and everything that had been on the mantelpiece and the dressing table was gone.

The doors of a small wardrobe, which matched the ugly shape of the dressing table, were open.

She saw that it was empty and she wondered if she would have to turn her gown inside-out again.

It would not be very fresh or pretty by this time.

She opened a door to the closet.

She could hardly believe it, but the closet had not been discovered and so it remained untouched.

All her luggage was there, including the beautiful gown that her mother had bought for her to wear at her Wedding.

She was just feeling a little disappointed that she could not have been married in it when a voice behind her said,

"This is exactly what you need for our Coronation."

She had not realised that the Prince had followed her into the room.

She smiled and said,

"I can look pretty for you after all. I was so afraid that all my lovely gowns would have gone."

"You look glorious just as you are now," he said, "but then I cannot wait to tell you very eloquently what I feel about you and I will certainly do so later."

He pulled her against him and kissed her, not gently, but fiercely, as if he had been afraid to lose her.

Almost before she could realise the wonder and excitement of his kiss, he had gone.

She heard him running down the passage to his own bedroom.

Gloria then turned to look at her clothes again.

They seemed to swim before her eyes.

And the sunshine streaming in through the windows was dazzling.

"We have – won! *We have – won*!" she wanted to cry out.

Then she knew that it was much more important than the fact that she would be the Queen of Arginos.

It was that she was now head over heels in love with the man she had married.

CHAPTER SEVEN

Gloria was still standing in the closet when she had heard somebody come into the room.

She turned round, thinking perhaps the Prince had returned, but then it was Delia, the maid who had looked after her when she arrived.

"You are all right, Delia?" Gloria exclaimed before she could speak. "You have not been hurt in any way?"

"No, my Lady, we was all in the cellar," the maid replied, "and, although they tried hard to break down the door, t'was too strong for them."

"I am glad about that," Gloria replied with a smile.

She thought too it was a good thing that the Revolutionaries could not get into the cellar to become drunk.

"The damage them people have done is terrible," Delia exclaimed. "All the curtains has gone and everythin' from your Ladyship's bedroom."

"But most of my clothes are still in the closet," Gloria answered.

"When we hears your Ladyship comin' and I sees you on the steps," the maid replied, "I goes and unlocks the door."

"So you locked it up," Gloria said. "That was very thoughtful and clever of you."

"I always keeps everythin' locked," Delia said as if she had been affronted. "And if I hadn't, you can be quite sure that those thieves would have taken every stitch your Ladyship owns."

Gloria looked again at the gown she was to have worn at her Wedding.

Then she said quietly,

"The Prince and I were married this morning, Delia, and I am thinking that, as he will be the King, I shall be able to wear this lovely gown at the Coronation."

Delia clasped her hands together.

"Oh, my La – I mean – Your Royal Highness, that is what we all want. Everyone in The Palace has always admired and loved Prince Darius and though 'tis terrible to speak ill of the dead, we'd not have been pleased to have the Crown Prince as our King."

She spoke almost as if she was going to burst into tears and Gloria said quickly,

"Then help me to change, Delia. His Royal Highness wants me downstairs and also, I am feeling hungry."

"There's nothin' – nothin' in The Palace to eat!" Delia exclaimed. "Those devils sacked the kitchen and the larders. You've never seen anythin' like the terrible mess they made."

"I expect the chefs will find something," Gloria replied, remembering the orders that the Prince had given.

She washed again in cold water and she thought that one really appreciated the luxury of a bath only when it was not possible to have one.

Despite Delia wanting to dress her in something really elaborate, she chose one of her simplest gowns.

It was white because she had nothing black in her trousseau to demonstrate that she was in mourning for the King.

But the white gown was most becoming and it made her look very young and pretty.

Delia brushed her hair until it shone.

While she was still doing so, they heard the Prince calling for her from outside the door,

"Hurry, Gloria, I am going down the stairs and I want you to come with me."

There was no chance of answering him then.

She heard his footsteps in the distance and next realised that the rugs that had covered the floor had also been removed by the intruders.

As Delia arranged her hair, Gloria thought that one thing was very obvious, they would have to buy some new curtains.

She would be able to have them in the spectrum of colours that she liked so much, not the dull ugly brown and beige which had prevailed in almost every room in The Palace.

At last Delia had finished with her hair.

It was only when she fastened her gown at the back that Gloria suddenly realised that all the jewellery she had brought with her had gone as well.

That was not really very important, but she said to Delia in a startled voice,

"Did those who sacked The Palace take the Crown Jewels?"

"Oh, no, Your Royal Highness," Delia replied. "They're not kept down here. They're in a special strong room in the Tower, which is near to the Houses of Parliament."

Gloria gave a sigh of relief.

If Darius was to be King, she really wanted him to look like one.

It would be ignominious for him to be crowned without a crown.

"The Queen's jewels be all in a safe," Delia went on. "I understands the men who comes here to snatch up everythin' they could broke the windows, but they was unable to get into the safe where they keeps the silver and all the jewels worn by the Queen."

Gloria was listening to this intently.

"I am glad about that," she said, "but why could they not get in?"

"There be two strong steel doors and, when we goes into the cellar, the Head Steward locks everythin' and takes all the keys away with him."

"So you had time when you knew that the Revolution was starting?"

"The soldiers held them back for a short time," Delia said, "and we was all hurried into the cellars. I comes up here to find you, but you wasn't here."

"That was very brave of you," Gloria exclaimed. "I was with His Royal Highness in the attic when somebody came to warn us. We changed our clothes swiftly and slipped down the back staircases."

"God was protecting you," Delia said. "And I prayed real hard they'd not kill Prince Darius."

"Your prayers were answered," Gloria said, "and both the Prince and I are very grateful to you."

"And you're married," Delia said as if she could hardly believe it, "without your pretty gown!"

Gloria smiled.

She was thinking of the strange little Church in which the Ceremony had taken place and how the Priest had no idea who they were.

They certainly had not looked like Royalty and she knew that she should be grateful that her crumpled plain gown had prevented her from being noticed and attacked.

She wondered if the Prince had been able to find something decent to wear.

When she went downstairs, she found him in the Throne Room, surrounded by people to whom he was giving orders.

He was also listening to complaints about the way the Revolutionaries had worked up the Arginosians into behaving aggressively.

"They were, of course, the young people," she heard a man say as she joined the Prince. "At the same time we cannot ignore the fact that it was the women who looted everything they could possibly carry."

"It happens in all Revolutions," the Prince said sadly, "but it gives us an excuse, as soon as things have settled down, to refurbish the Palace and make it very much more cheerful than it is now."

The man looked at him in surprise.

But Gloria understood and she slipped her hand into the Prince's.

She was relieved to see that he was wearing a white Military tunic just like the one he had worn on her first night at dinner.

Also the black trousers with their bright red stripe.

He wore, however, no decorations.

As if he knew what she was thinking, he said,

"You will not be surprised to hear that all my clothes have been taken from my room. What I have

~170~

on was, fortunately, together with another suit, being pressed by my valet."

"It is certainly more appropriate to the occasion than what you were wearing when you arrived," Gloria remarked.

"And I can say the same for you," the Prince answered.

He dropped his voice before he added,

"You look even lovelier than you did this morning when I kissed you."

Gloria blushed.

At the same time her fingers tightened on his.

She knew that she wanted more than anything else that he should kiss her again and yet again.

With an effort he released her hand and turned to the men who were waiting to speak to him.

As she listened to him, Gloria became aware that he seemed to have grown in stature.

He also had an authority about him that had not been there before.

He was listening intently to detailed reports of all that had happened in the City during the Revolution.

They were actually not really so devastating as he had feared.

A number of shops had been looted, mostly those that sold food or wine.

The windows had been smashed in the Houses of Parliament, but nothing had been set on fire fortunately.

Listening, Gloria realised that the Revolutionaries had been trying to entice more people to riot just when they had arrived in the Square.

"I understand, Your Royal Highness," one man said, "that the Russians had not expected Lady Gloria to arrive so speedily from England. They have sent for reinforcements that have not yet arrived. Therefore the number of foreigners in the country is comparatively small at this moment."

"Very small indeed, if we recall that a considerable number have been killed," Captain Makius interposed.

"If there are any left, I am sure you can cope with them," the Prince said to him.

The two men smiled at each other.

Then there was a long wait before there was any sign of food and Gloria was getting very hungry.

However, she was intensely interested in everything that the Prince was doing and saying to his soldiers

Although he had spent most of his time abroad, it was very obvious that he well knew who had ideas like his own for modernising the country.

Every minute they were in the Throne Room more Government Officials began to arrive to report on what was happening in the City and in the countryside.

They were not the old men who she had encountered on her arrival.

They had gone into hiding, while the younger men had brought reports from the various Departments of State to the Prince.

The Prince told each one of them what was wanted and who would be in authority to give orders

He had then chosen the Prime Minister, the Minister of State for Foreign Affairs and the Home Secretary while they were talking to him.

He also explained, to their astonishment, that Captain Makius was now taking over as the new Commander-in-Chief of the Army.

Then he announced that a young Lieutenant-Commander of his acquaintance was to hold the rank of Admiral and to take over command of the Navy.

He was amazed when the Prince promoted him as it was the last thing that he might have expected

Watching everything that was going on, Gloria thought it a pity that the expressions on their faces could not be recorded for future posterity.

The sun was no longer shining through the windows and it was very much colder than it had been earlier on in the day.

At last servants came to say that the Prince's orders had been carried out and there was food for everybody ready in the dining room.

The Prince invited those who had just been appointed to senior positions to join them.

Offering Gloria his arm, he led her from the Throne Room into the hall and then on to the dining room.

The chefs had obviously worked miracles to procure the feast laid out before them.

Although there was a great deal of *Moussaka,* the delicious Greek speciality, there were also a number of other dishes and massive bowls of fruit.

A table had been arranged for Prince Darius and Gloria at one end of the room.

There were a number of other tables, some large and some small, but it was obvious, however, that the majority of those who had filed into the room would have to stand.

They seemed quite content to do so and were chatting away to each other animatedly.

There were servants, in various stages of dress, to pour out the wine.

Those who had managed to hide in the cellar from the Revolutionaries were fortunately in uniform.

A large number had, however, run out of The Palace as they were and then returned to find that everything they possessed had disappeared.

Gloria found that the *Moussaka* was just what she needed at that particular moment.

She was so hungry, having had nothing since breakfast, that she ate in silence, aware that the Prince was doing the same.

Only when they had both asked for a second helping did he say with a smile,

"This is indeed a very unusual Wedding breakfast, my darling one, but then everything so far has been very different from what you might have imagined."

"Very very different," she responded in a soft voice.

As she spoke, she looked into his eyes.

He knew at once that she was telling him how much she loved him.

And that was certainly something she had not expected when she had hated him all the way from England to Arginos.

He put out both his hands to touch hers.

Before he could speak, there was somebody else arriving to tell him what was happening in the City.

"Everyone is coming back to the City, Your Royal Highness," he said. "The shopkeepers are already trying to repair the damage."

His eyes twinkled as he finished,

"And making out extra large bills for compensation after what Your Royal Highness has generously told them!"

"What we have to do," the Prince said, "is to get everything back to normal. Then we can commence our programme for prosperity. I want your reports on which men are particularly good at planting new vineyards. And I want cargo ships built immediately that can carry our produce to Constantinople and other big Cities."

The man who he was speaking to put up his hands as if he could hardly contemplate such ideas.

At the same time he was smiling and his eyes were shining.

'He is waking them up,' Gloria thought, 'and that is exactly what is wanted here.'

Captain Makius arranged for the soldiers to come to the buffet, a dozen at a time, after the more senior Officers had helped themselves.

They were obviously somewhat overwhelmed to find themselves eating in The Palace.

The Prince, however, put them entirely at their ease with his jokes.

Gloria realised that he was already a hero in their eyes and growing in stature all the time.

She had heard him tell Captain Makius that, if any man had been killed or wounded, his wife and family would be looked after and given a pension.

It seemed to her extraordinary that having lived as he had, not being allowed to play any part in the running of the Kingdom, he was aware of every detail that was of importance.

'He is wonderful!' she said to herself again and again.

They finished eating and there was very little left of the large buffet.

Captain Makius, who had left the room, came back to say,

"I think, Your Royal Highness, that you should make an appearance outside The Palace. An enormous crowd is gathered there and they are wishing to cheer you."

"Then, of course, they must see us," the Prince agreed.

He put out his hand to Gloria.

As she took it, she realised that Captain Makius was looking anxious.

The Prince must have been aware of it too because he asked,

"Do you think there will be any danger?"

"I sincerely hope not, Your Royal Highness," the Captain replied. "I have already told my men to watch the crowd and to shoot straight if any Russian attempts to destroy you."

Gloria gave a little cry and the Prince said rapidly,

"It is a risk we have to take, but I am sure, Makius, that your men will be as efficient as they have been already."

He and Gloria then walked from the dining room towards The Palace entrance.

Now Gloria could hear the loud shouts and cheers of the crowd.

She thought it sounded as if they were happy and amused.

It was a very different sound from that of the hostile Revolutionaries they had seen when they were escaping.

A footman opened the door for them and, as they stepped out onto the top of the steps, there was a deafening roar of applause from below.

The sun was sinking in a crimson glory, its light glistening on the tops of the trees.

It also illuminated the Prince and Gloria as they stood just outside The Palace doors.

It made them look like people from a Fairytale.

Gloria felt, as they moved slowly down the steps, as if she had stepped out into a fantasy world.

The crowd roared, shouted and waved with obvious exhilaration and joy.

The Prince stopped and told the soldiers who were keeping back the crowd from joining them on the steps to sit down.

They were surprised at the order and for a moment did not obey it.

Then, as Captain Makius repeated it, they sat down directly in front of them.

Other soldiers stood on opposite sides of the steps, watching the crowds with their rifles at the ready.

The Prince waited awhile until there was complete silence.

Then he began,

"Thank you very much for coming here and assuring me of your loyalty and assistance in making our country up to date and modern.

"I cannot do it without you. That means that every man, woman and child has to strive, as I shall be doing, towards peace and prosperity. What my wife wants more than anything else is that this should be a happy country and that is what we intend to make it."

There was a roar of applause as he finished.

Then somebody shouted,

"The Queen! *The Queen*! Let the Queen speak!"

Gloria looked at Darius and he said,

"Of course. If that is what they want."

He raised his hand for silence and, raising her voice, Gloria started to speak,

"I came here, at the wish of Her Majesty Queen Victoria, expressly to help you and I have already come to love this country. I think that you are all wonderful, as is my husband. I know that, if the women are willing to help me, we can do what he wants, not with guns and cannon but with Love."

There was a little pause as Gloria finished speaking.

Then the whole company shouted, cheered and threw flowers over the heads of the soldiers so that they fell at her feet.

The Prince picked up one of them and handed it to her and that made them cheer even louder.

Then Darius and Gloria moved slowly back up the steps.

They stopped three times to wave and acknowledge the cheering crowds before they had reached the top.

As they went inside The Palace, the crowd then sang the National Anthem before they gradually began to disperse.

Inside, Gloria said,

"They love you already and it makes me – want to cry."

"That is something you are forbidden to do on your Wedding Day!" the Prince smiled.

The way he spoke made Gloria give a little laugh.

"Who has ever had such a strange – Wedding Day?" she asked. "Or such a dangerous Marriage!"

"And a very exhausting one," the Prince added. "You are to go up to bed and I will join you as soon as I can. If you have fallen asleep, I will kiss you and go on kissing you until you wake up."

The way he spoke, in a voice that only Gloria could hear, made her blush.

He kissed her hand and she felt his lips surge against the softness of her skin.

With difficulty she forced herself away from him and went up the stairs.

She could not help wishing that the room was more attractive and was not without any curtains or blankets on the bed.

She opened the door and then gave a little gasp.

There were still no curtains at the windows, but the bed had been made up with lace-edged sheets and a white satin cover.

Everywhere in the room there were flowers of every size and colour and the air was hugely fragrant with them.

Gloria stood still.

She thought that only Darius, in the midst of all he had to do, would remember that she loved flowers of all colours and fragrances.

He knew that she thought the room she had slept in when she arrived at The Palace was very ugly and depressing.

'How can any man be so marvellous?' Gloria asked herself.

Then, as Delia came hurrying from the closet where she had been tidying the clothes that had not been stolen, Gloria asked her,

"Where have all these wonderful flowers arrived from?"

"His Royal Highness ordered that every flower and pot that had not been stolen was to be brought in here," Delia replied, "and I knew that Your Ladysh – I mean – Your Royal Highness, would be pleased with them."

"Pleased," Gloria exclaimed. "It is a bower of beauty. How could I not be delighted that the Prince would think of me in such a flattering way?"

"You'll make a great King, Your Royal Highness," Delia said. "Everyone's sayin' so and I never heard anythin' like all those cheers from such a great crowd of people!"

Gloria let her undo her gown.

Then, to her relief, Delia produced one of the very pretty nightgowns that her mother had bought for her in Bond Street.

"I was so afraid that this was one of the things that might have been stolen," she said.

"They took some of the garments," Delia replied, "but, fortunately, I put only some of your lovely lingerie into the drawers in the bedroom and the rest were all packed into the closet."

"I shall bless that closet every day of my life!," Gloria laughed. "And you, Delia, for being clever enough to lock it up."

"I'm sorry there be no curtains. Your Royal Highness," Delia said, "the stars may keep you awake."

'They will not do that," Gloria grinned.

"Then God bless Your Royal Highness," Delia said, "and may you always and for ever be as happy as you and His Royal Highness are today."

"We will be," Gloria said confidently.

When Delia left, Gloria lay back against the pillows, gazing up at the stars.

There was only one candle left beside the bed as the rest had been stolen.

She thought that the moonlight shining through the windows was very romantic.

It made the room with its fragrant flowers seem part of a celestial dream.

How, she asked herself, could everything that had happened since she had left London be anything else?

She recalled how she had hated the Prince while she was on the British Battleship.

Every day it brought her nearer and nearer to a marriage that she felt would destroy her and make her miserable for the rest of her life.

Instead the Prince had been entirely different from what she could have anticipated in her wildest dreams.

Now that she had thought about it, she might have known from the first moment that it would be impossible not to fall in love with him.

He was just so handsome, so masculine and so very attractive, but it was something more than that.

There was a fine spiritual link between them, which she knew was deeper than just the attraction of a man for a woman.

It made her sure that they had known each other in many previous lives and had now met and had fallen in love again in this one.

She had always believed that the Universe was powered by love and those truly in love always came back to each other through time and space.

It was something that she had first learnt from books, but had never thought that it would apply to her personally.

Now, when she felt the vibrations of the Prince linked with hers, she knew for certain that they already were an indivisible part of each other.

It was something that seemingly could not have happened in the very short time that they had known each other.

It was what the Chinese called '*the world behind the world*' where they had met so many times before.

'I love him,' Gloria said to the stars, 'and, as you have brought us together, you must help us never to lose our love, but to increase it, year by year and perhaps from this life into another yet one.'

It was something that she had indeed thought of before.

And now it seemed as real to her as the undisputed fact that she was the Prince's wife.

She knew his most intimate thoughts and feelings and they were also hers.

'I love him!' she murmured to herself again.

As she spoke, the communicating door to the sitting room opened and then the Prince came in.

His head and shoulders were silhouetted against the stars, but she could see that he was smiling and looking very happy.

Her eyes seemed dazzled as he came towards her.

He reached her and sat down on the side of the bed gazing at her overwhelming beauty.

Now, by the light of the single flickering candle, she could see him clearly.

Her eyes seemed to fill her small face completely and the gold of her hair shimmered over her shoulders.

Neither of them spoke.

They just stared at each other.

Then he asked her,

"Have you any idea how beautiful you are?"

"Th-that is what I – want you to – think."

"You are also very brave," he went on. "No other woman in the world would have been as magnificent as you were today in circumstances which would have made them hysterical with fear."

"I-I was with – you," Gloria murmured, "that was – all that mattered."

"How could I have guessed, when they told me that I was to marry an English girl to save my country, that she would be the very Goddess who has always been in a Shrine in my heart, but I had never thought to find in this dimension?"

"I was just thinking – before you came in," Gloria whispered, "that we, the two of us, must have – known each other in many other lives – and now – we have found each other – again."

He understood, as she knew that no other man would have done.

"I was always aware that you were somewhere in the world," he said quietly, "but I was so afraid that I would never find you."

"And now – you have."

"You are mine," he said, "and I intend to tell you in great detail how much you mean to me."

He bent forward as he spoke and blew out the candle.

Then he went round to the other side of the bed and got into it.

As he took Gloria into his arms, she felt a wild excitement moving within her breast.

It was an ecstasy beyond description and beyond thought.

All she knew was that this was Love.

Overpowering and overwhelming.

Now they were both being swept away by it like a rushing avalanche.

The stars glittered and gleamed through the window, touching everything with a silver light.

As the Prince took possession of her lips, Gloria felt as if they were moving inside her heart.

She was not certain if they spoke or if the word '*Love*' just vibrated between them.

It was all part of the Prince's kiss, the touch of his hands and the ecstasy that made her body melt into his.

"You are mine," he said again. "Mine for all Eternity and I will never, my perfect and precious little wife, lose you."

Then he was kissing her fiercely, demandingly and passionately, until, as he made Gloria his, they both touched the stars.

They had found Love, the Love that was Eternal and Divine.

It would be theirs for as long as they lived in this life and beyond.